ALSO BY SAM LEE JACKSON

The Jackson Blackhawk Series

The Girl at the Deep End of the Lake
The Librarian, Her Daughter and the Man Who Lost His Head.
The Bag Lady, the Boat Bum, and the West Side King
They Called Her Indigo
The Darker Hours
The Colonel, the Cove and the Dog that didn't Bark
The Man with the Lightning Scar

Westerns
Shonto's Kid
Shadow Dancer

Enjoy all of Sam Lee Jackson's exciting novels at
samleejackson.com

SHADOW DANCER

SAM LEE JACKSON

Shadow Dancer

Piping Rock Publications
3608 E Taro Lane. Phoenix AZ 85050
www.samleejackson.com

ISBN 978-1-7351654-3-1 (Print)
ISBN 978-1-7351654-4-8 (E)
Library of Congress Control Number 2021924219

Acknowledgements

I give thanks for my team.
Thanks to my painstaking editor, Ann Hedrick and my
amazing cover illustrator Ladybird.
And of course, family is everything.
Especially Carol. The beacon on my rocky shores.

Shadow Dancer is based on true events that took place in the Arizona Territory between 1879 and 1886. It was during the time of the last of the Indian campaigns when the ferocious warlike Apaches were finally subdued. For the sake of entertainment, the principal characters of this book are fictitious but the events that led up to the massacre at Cibicue Creek are largely accurate thanks to a wonderful book titled *Apache Days and After*, penned by Thomas Cruse, Brigadier General, U.S. Army retired. General Cruse lived these events as a young officer assigned to Fort Apache, Arizona Territory.

This novel is a work of fiction, but without General Cruse's historical facts, it wouldn't be what it is.

sam lee Jackson

1

The old man leaned against the mud and stick wall of his wickiup, his eyes closed, as he soaked in the heat of the father sun. The warmth helped his old aching bones. Even with his eyes closed he knew who the rider was as he listened to the man make his way up the hill on horseback. It had been a long time since this man had been to see Ochocama. He knew why he was coming.

The young man rode through the camp, coming directly to the old warrior. The women stopped their work long enough to watch him pass by. He rode with an arrogance that he had carried his whole life. The man pulled his pony to a halt in front of the old man. The old man appeared to be sleeping. The man sat looking at him. He might be asleep and then he might not.

The old man knew the impatience of this young one. He had known him his whole life. He knew the boy wouldn't wait long. He was right.

The young man rubbed a finger across the deep scar that slashed across his face. "Shid'ale," he finally said.

Ochocama opened his eyes. The young man had grown. He had grown physically and in stature in the tribes and he knew this young man's arrogance didn't allow him to respect the old ways the way he should.

The young man didn't wait for a response. "I have come a long way, old man. I am Gar."

The old man waved a hand, as if shooing a fly. "I know who you are," he said. He took the staff that was leaning beside him and pushed himself to his feet.

"I know who you are," he said again. He looked up into the face of the young man. "You still carry the scar you received when Ugashe' saved your life."

Gar snorted. "Ugashe' did not save my life."

"You are still alive," Ochocama said simply. He turned to look for old Nino. She was his youngest sister. The last of his family. After losing her husband to the hair-face soldiers she had come back to Ochocama's lodge to care for him.

She was close by. She saw him looking and came to him. He waved a hand and she turned to get tulipi and something from the cook pot. They rarely needed verbal communication. He looked up at the young man. "Climb down and we will eat and drink."

"I don't have time," the young man said.

This angered Ochocama, but he didn't let it show. "You forget your manners," he said. "Tell me of my old friend Noch-ay-del-Klinne."

Without waiting, the old man, leaning on his staff, made his way to the shade of a tall juniper. He sat in the nettles, shifting until he was comfortable. Gar was watching him, fighting the anger he felt inside. He knew this old man was important to the shaman Noch-ay-del-Klinne. The old man ignored him until he was comfortable, and Nino brought food and drink. Finally, Ochocama looked up at the younger man and waved a hand indicating the man should sit beside him. Gar reluctantly slid from his pony and sat. He took a piece of meat and took the tin cup Nino offered him. He sipped it, knowing he had to if he were to accomplish what he had come for.

"How is my old friend, Noch-ay-del-Klinne?"

"He has seen a vision," Gar said, glad to be getting to it.

Ochocama said, "Yes, the vision. We have all heard of this vision. Even the hair-faces have heard of this vision."

"Noch-ay-del-Klinne dances the shadow dance and wears the ghost shirt. His vision says the whites will fall before him and our dead shall rise to fight and anyone with the ghost shirt cannot be harmed."

Ochocama sat for a long time. He finally looked at Gar. His eyes were tired.

"This is a very powerful vision," he said slowly. "So powerful that I wonder why my old friend has sent you to me? What could he need from me?"

This is the question Gar had been rehearsing the answer for all the way here.

He spoke the words he had rehearsed. "Noch-ay-del-Klinne wants to come to your rancheria and perform the shadow dance. If Ochocama dances with Noch-ay-del-Klinne, all the people will dance."

"If Noch-ay-del-Klinne thinks I am free, he is mistaken. The hair-face chief Nantan Lupan and his scouts could find me anytime. I am not worth their trouble. We don't bother the hair-face. Not the ranchers or farmers. If my people raid, they do it far south. I am trying to live my last days resting in the light of father sun and drinking tulipi until I am drunk enough to sleep."

Gar knew this was true but, he wasn't really here to ask permission. He was here to tell Ochocama that Noch-ay-del-Klinne was on his way. And when he arrived, he would dance. And Ochocama's people would dance. And Ochocama would have to dance.

The old chief set his cup of tulipi aside. His appetite was gone. He had known Noch-ay-del-Klinne would come the first day he had heard of the vision. He also knew when Noch-ay-del-Klinne left the reservation the hair-face soldiers would follow to take him back. Ochocama knew that when Noch-ay-del-Klinne came, his own days of freedom would be numbered.

He looked at Gar. "Who would come with my old friend?"

"His daughter Nalin, me and a few others, to protect him on his journey."

Ochocama struggled to his feet, leaning heavily on his staff.

"Tell my old friend I am always happy to welcome him to my rancheria."

Triumphantly, Gar went to his pony and mounted and rode away without looking back. Ochocama watched him until he was no longer in sight. Ochocama turned and old Nino was watching him.

"Bring my medicine pouch," he said.

Nino obediently went inside the wickiup and rummaged through a pile of blankets. She found the soft leather pouch made by Ochocama's grandmother. She spread a blanket and lay it in the middle. She left the wickiup.

A few minutes later, Ochocama came in and took the pouch in his hands. He sank to his knees and began to chant.

2

John Daisy really didn't like stopping at Stolvig's Station, but it was the only place for miles where you could trade half-broke ponies and haunches of venison for whiskey, powder and possibles. John Daisy didn't care about the whiskey. Ugashe', his white brother the whites called Kid, rarely drank any himself. But he usually carried some for trading. He complained that Stolvig carried two kinds of whiskey. Crap and shit. You could also get staples like sugar and flour, lard and fatback. The reason for this was that the Army patrols regularly stopped here.

One had stopped here an hour ago. John Daisy had been lounging on the porch while the Kid was inside passing the time and gossip with Stolvig. Some of the troopers had given John Daisy a hard look as they went inside. Fortunately for them they were in a hurry to get in and drink beer, whiskey and play cards. The civilian scout was followed by an Apache from the reservation. They had hesitated and stared at him, but John Daisy ignored them. The Apache nodded and began to speak. Booker didn't understand a word, so he went inside. John Daisy knew the Apache's name was Manuelito. As the Apache spoke,

John Daisy slowly raised his eyes to look at the man. He listened intently. The man finished and abruptly went inside.

The sun had moved and was now directly on John Daisy and he decided to go inside where it was cooler. He knew they would be there a while with Ugashe' having fresh suckers to play poker with. The inside was one big room with a plank bar running down one side. Coming from the bright outside, it was dark inside. The imperfect walls had chinks and holes, and shafts of light illuminated dust motes that floated in the air.

John Daisy moved to a corner of the room and sat in a chair that rested against the wall. He tipped his flat-brimmed hat down over his eyes and watched the white child play cards with the soldiers. He could tell the Kid was winning and knew their stay at the station would probably last as long as the Kid had card players. The Kid had learned much from the old gunfighter, Shonto Page, and the old man had considered poker one of the educational essentials.

The soldiers not playing cards were at the bar drinking. Manuelito had kept apart but now came and stood beside the civilian scout. He spoke to Stolvig, his voice so soft John Daisy couldn't make out what was said. But he knew the Apache had asked for a whiskey.

Stolvig would sell a piece of his grandmother's ass for two bits but for some reason he decided to show off for the blue-bellies.

"Booker," he said to the civilian scout. "You know I don't sell whiskey to no niggers. Red or black."

Booker looked at him. Manuelito looked at Booker, expecting him to intervene. "He just wants a drink," Booker said.

Stolvig looked at the Apache. "No whiskey!"

John Daisy was bored so he stood and moved to the bar. He laid his rifle on the top. "I'd like a beer," he said.

The soldiers at the bar turned to look at him. Booker looked surprised.

"I just told him no whiskey," Stolvig said. "I can't sell you a beer."

"Okay," John Daisy said. "Give me one then."

Stolvig stuttered, "I-I just said I don't serve Indians."

"No," John Daisy said. "What you said was you don't sell to niggers." He looked at the Apache next to him. "He's not a nigger. He's White Mountain. I'm not a nigger. I am a Coyotero. My father was Alchesay. My grandfather is Ochocama. And I would like a beer."

Stolvig looked across the room to the Kid, who seemed engrossed in his cards. "Kid, I don't want no trouble," Stolvig said.

After a long moment the Kid looked up, his pale eyes untroubled. "Well, then I suggest you give him a beer."

Manuelito looked at Stolvig and spit on the floor. He then spit out a long string of words, heavy with scorn. He turned abruptly and went out the door.

One of the soldiers said, "What did he say?"

"Beats me," Booker said. "I never did learn that gibberish."

John Daisy looked at the soldier, "He said when the dancing starts his people will own it all again." No sense telling them what Manuelito had said about the ghost shirts.

"What the hell does that mean?"

John Daisy ignored that and looked at Stolvig. "I'd like a beer," he said.

Stolvig stood for a long moment. He looked over to the Kid. The Kid was looking at John Daisy. "Well, shit," Stolvig said.

Booker turned and looked at the Kid. "I've heard of you," Booker said. "They say you shot Long Bedeaux over at Delnorte's station."

The Kid turned back to his cards. He made a bet. He didn't say anything. His opponent folded. The Kid pulled in the coins from the center of the table.

Booker continued, "I knew Long Bedeaux and he was a mighty hard man. If you took him, you have to have some hard bark on you."

The Kid sighed. He looked up at Booker, his eyes the color of water. "He was threatening some friends of mine."

The Kid looked at Stolvig. He said, "Stolvig, you oughta know that John Daisy don't even like your beer. If I was you, I'd offer him one on the house."

Stolvig knew he had lost. He stepped to the keg and drew the beer and walked it down to John Daisy. He set it on the bar in front of him. "How 'bout a beer on the house?"

John Daisy lifted his rifle off the bar. He smiled broadly, "No thanks. I gotta be goin'." He looked at the Kid, "You coming?"

Booker said to the Kid, "Stick around, I'll buy you a drink."

The Kid lay his cards face down, the game spoiled now. He started stacking up his coins.

"Some say you was raised by Shonto Page. That so?" Booker said, leaning an elbow on the bar.

The Kid stood up and reaching behind him, brought his hat up on his head. Now he turned to the scout. "He was my friend." he said simply. The two men's eyes were locked for a long moment and Stolvig felt relief at the center of attention shifting.

The big scout nodded then turned back to his drink. "Met him once," he said. "Damn good man."

The tension left the air and Stolvig was left standing with John Daisy's black eyes back on him. The bluster was gone, and he turned again to the Kid. "I don't want no trouble," he said to the room at large.

Holding the rifle easily, John Daisy moved down the room toward the door. The Kid stepped away from the table and moved right behind. As they reached the door Booker said, "They say Shonto Page was the best shot that ever lived. Are you as good as he was?"

In one fluid moment the Kid turned, drew and fired before the echo of the words hit the walls. The beer glass that Stolvig had set on the bar exploded. The separated handle hit the floor and skittered across it. On the heels of the first explosion was another one and the handle disappeared into tiny fragments.

The sudden silence lay on the room like dust on a blanket. John Daisy levered another shell into his rifle.

"Not even by half," the Kid said. They turned and went out into the bright sunlight.

As the Kid followed John Daisy out to the horses he said, "Goddammit, why do you always pull this shit when I'm winning?"

3

It was into the summer, and in the high desert it was dry with dust covering everything at the slightest breeze. The Kid felt that they had tarried too long in the hot desert valleys and wanted to head for the cooler high pines. They were traveling light, as usual. They had even sold Stolvig their pack horse.

John Daisy rode the big, spotted appaloosa he favored. The Kid teased him about the horse. He said it was against the nature and the character of a Dinee not to ride a horse to death then eat it.

John Daisy called this horse, *Shilah*, sister. Despite the teasing, the appaloosa was the best piece of horse flesh in the territory. The only other female animal on God's earth that might hold some competition in John Daisy's breast was Nalin, the daughter of the medicine man Noch-ay-del-Klinne. The girl they had been raised with. The one John Daisy still mooned over. The one that John Daisy and every other young man had tried to court, going so far as to leave ponies at the door to Noch-ay-del-Klinne's wickiup, only to have them returned the next morning. Finally, Nalin had to make it clear, she had no intention of marriage as long as her widowed father was alive. He was the most important medicine man in all the tribes, and she served only him.

As soon as her name came up, the Kid threw aside any hope of getting as far north as he wanted. Riding along at an easy pace, a piece of weed hanging from his mouth, John Daisy said mildly, "Manuelito says that Nalin and her father are headed to Ochocama's."

"Who's Manuelito?"

"That Dinee scout at Stolvigs."

They stepped along in silence a moment, then the Kid said, "Means they're going off the reservation. It means they will lead Crook straight to Ochocama's."

John Daisy grunted. "Crook knows where Ochocama is."

"Yeah, but up to now, Crook has left Ochocama alone. If Noch-ay-del-Klinne goes there, people will follow. He can't ignore that," the Kid continued, one leg hooked over the pommel while he rolled a cigarette. "Why the hell would Noch-ay-del-Klinne do somethin' like that?"

"Manuelito said that Noch-ay-del-Klinne has had a vision. He wants to hold the Shadow Dances."

"I thought that was long dead. Why Ochocama? Why not pick a canyon somewhere and go and dance there?"

John Daisy spit the weed out. "Ochocama has much prestige. And Ochocama is his old friend. If Ochocama dances with the spirits, so will all the people."

"So, we are going to Ochocama's?" the Kid asked, swinging his leg down and blowing smoke into the dry still air.

The hills were long sloping, rolling hills and they had reached the tallest crest of one. John Daisy pulled the appaloosa to a halt. "There will be trouble," he said. " Ochocama is old now. He could need his grandsons."

The Kid nodded, "Yeah, could be." He looked at John Daisy. "Or maybe you just wanna see Nalin again. See if you can change her mind."

John Daisy snorted in feigned disgust, then with a whoop, he kicked the appaloosa, and they took off a hellin' down the slope.The Kid just shook his head and followed John Daisy down the hill. Thinking of Nalin brought back memories of his time in Ochocama's rancheria. Unlike all the other boys, it had taken a while for him to notice Nalin.

He had come to live with Ochocama after Shonto Page had been killed. He had been there for two summers before he really noticed the young woman the older men called the butterfly. She had transformed from a gangly, knobby, girl child with too many teeth and head too big for the scrawny body, into a striking, beautiful woman. It was quite a transformation. The kind of beauty that comes along in the tribes once in a lifetime. The older women compared her to Ana, the third wife of Mangus Coloradas, a legendary beauty. Some said this didn't count because Ana was Nakaiye. Mexican.

There was great speculation as to which lodge Nalin would end up in, but her father, Noch-ay-del-Klinne, turned away all suitors and it became obvious he intended for her to stay and tend to him. The old women thought this was a shame and a waste. If she waited too long, her belly would never hold a child.

All the young men thought it was a waste also. All but the Kid, who was called Ugashe'. He was so curious and inquisitive

12

that he could become a pest to the older men as they sat in council. They would wave him away. "Ugashe'! Ugashe'! Go away. Get out!" It became his name.

Chan Deisi's biggest rival in the camp was a boy a year older, named Gar. Gar excelled at all the sports and easily beat all the other boys in the games they played. Except Chan Deisi. Chan Deisi came in a close second a lot, but sometimes, by sheer grit, he would best Gar. Gar hated him for it. He also hated the white child, Ugashe'. If asked why, he couldn't explain it. Something about the boy's complete self-confidence and the fact that Ochocama seemed to favor the white boy. But of all the emotions the young Gar experienced, none was stronger than the lust he felt for Nalin.

Gar was obsessed by Nalin, and this came to a head the summer the Bronco came. Every great once in a while a man would be so unspeakably evil that even his tribe couldn't condone him. The elders would cast him out. These bad men were called *Broncos*. They were outcasts. They belonged to no tribe. They roamed the territory, stealing and murdering. Sometimes they would band together and raid both sides of the border. The whites called them Comancheros. The Bronco that came to Ochocama's that year came alone.

He knew the rancheria was there, there was much sign. He just wanted to steal a horse and food. Maybe a good weapon if he could find one. What he found was Nalin.

He was a big man, thick and muscled in the chest which was crisscrossed with scars. He had caused much trouble in his rancheria. He had stolen another man's wife and was forced to pay for her. Then he stole the man's horse and was caught. The tribal police had whipped him until he was unconscious. He was banished by the council and had been dragged out of the rancheria, into the desert and left for dead. He didn't die. He lay in the desert for two days until he got some strength back. Then he stealthily came back into the rancheria. Silent as a ghost he made his way into his punisher's wickiup and slit the throat of everyone sleeping there. He stole the same horse again, took food and weapons and rode away.

In the last days, he had seen enough sign to know there was a rancheria close. This was unusual. Most of the tribes had been forced onto the reservation. The first he saw of Nalin was her bare footprint etched into the soft loam next to the creek that was thick with overflow. He had planned to sleep next to the water, then steal into the rancheria and take a horse. His had given out two days ago. He had taken the time to feast on it, then put meat in his leather pouch and started walking. But now, the footprint changed everything. It had been a long while since he had lain with a woman. When he was finished with her, he could sell her to the Comancheros.

The Bronco slowly moved up the bank and made his way cautiously through the trees. The creek took a bend about fifty yards ahead and as he drew closer, he suddenly sensed movement on the other side of the stand of trees. He silently moved to a better vantage. On the other side, the creek collected into a natural pool. At the pool was a young girl. A tall young girl.

The girl was balanced on one foot while the other tested the water. She reached with both hands and untied the colorful scrap of cloth she was wearing to hold her hair. She placed it carefully on the ground. She reached down, grasped the hem of her shapeless dress and smoothly pulled it up and over her head. She tossed it aside. She stood for a moment, her naked body in the sunlight, running her fingers through her long black hair.

The Bronco sucked in a silent breath, Her body was not like other women, but taller and slimmer, her breasts small but well formed. She squatted suddenly then slipped into the chilled water. The Bronco put his hand on the handle of his knife and started silently forward.

4

In his youth Gar had rapidly approached the age when a man starts thinking of having his own woman. He arrogantly assumed that woman would be the daughter of Noch-ay-del-Klinne, the seer. She was the most beautiful girl in the camp. Probably in all of Apacheria. So, he naturally assumed she should be his.

He knew her father had spurned other offers, saying she was too young, so when he saw her leaving the camp, he thought it would be a good opportunity to accidently run into her. They could talk. At their age, socialization between the sexes was frowned upon, but accidents happen. He had no doubt if she got to know him, she would see him as the best choice for a mate.

He watched with interest as she went off on her own. He knew she was heading for the creek that rushed its waters through the red rock country. He knew of the special pool the women used to bathe in and wash the family clothes in. The men in the camp avoided this pool, giving the women their place.

Gar hurried out of the camp as nonchalantly as possible.

There was a ridge behind the encampment, and it was just luck that Chan Deisi and the Kid were at the top. They had been hunting ground squirrels when Chan Deisi touched the Kid's arm and pointed downward.

"Where's he going?" the Kid said.

Chan Deisi pointed again. This time at the distant figure of Nalin disappearing into the creek bottom. Chan Deisi laughed and started down.

"Where are you going," the Kid said.

Chan Deisi kept moving without replying. The Kid shrugged and followed. Everyone knew where the pool was. It was logical the girl was heading for it. If so, there was no need to keep Gar or Nalin in sight. Chan Deisi was moving rapidly. Irritated at this nonsense, the Kid followed.

Gar moved along the creek bed, rehearsing in his mind the innocence he would portray when he accidently ran into the girl. He climbed down a drop and crossed over to the other side. There was easier footing there. He rounded an outcropping and there Nalin stood thirty yards away. She was removing her buckskin dress. She dropped it to the ground. His breath caught and he ducked back. If she saw him now, she would never talk to him. He cautiously peered through thick branches of a creosote bush. Nalin was in the water. She began swimming. She was coming directly at him.

He began to silently back away, slowly, step by step backing around the large boulder. He stopped, his heart pounding. He leaned against the cool rock. He listened intently to her splashing sounds, ready to bolt if he thought he would be discovered. The sounds below remained normal and after a few moments he cautiously peered around and down toward the pool.

Terror seized his throat. Nalin stood in the shallows, gazing downstream, away from him, twisting the water from her hair. Creeping up behind her, knife in hand, was a big, scarred man. A stranger. Gar was frozen, unable to move. In that instant, Nalin heard the whisper of moccasin on the rock behind her. She turned suddenly, then bolted, quick as a deer toward the bank. The man was too fast. He grabbed a handful of hair and swung her around. She began a scream, but it was cut short by the clubbed fist that knocked her senseless. She fell, limp, held up only by the man's grip on her hair.

The Bronco put the knife away, looking around. Pulling her body up, he slung her nude body over his shoulder and started picking his way across the stream.

Gar finally moved. Numbed, he stepped out from hiding, not knowing what to do. He knew he was no match for this man. The man caught the movement up the bank and swung around. He looked directly at the young boy who stood transfixed above him. He looked around for others. In an instant he knew the boy was alone. With a cold and evil grin, he pulled his knife and sliced it across Nalin's buttock. It was not a deep cut, but the blood began to run.

The man laughed out loud. Gar turned and bolted back toward the camp.

5

The Kid and John Daisy were almost to the creek bottom when Gar burst out of the underbrush. He looked frantic. He skidded to a stop, out of breath.

"Nalin," he managed to gasp.

"Where is she," John Daisy said, alarmed at Gar's obvious agitation.

"A Bronco," Gar stuttered. "A stranger. He has taken her. We have to get help."

"There is no time," John Daisy said. "Which way?"

Gar pointed down the creek. The Kid started forward followed by John Daisy. Gar stood surprised, then moved quickly after. The rushing waters muted all the sound. In a few minutes they reached Nalin's dress lying on the ground. John Daisy picked it up and looked at it for blood. He stuffed it into his belt. The Kid was looking all around.

"This way," Gar said, moving off. The Kid studied the ground for a moment. Satisfied, he moved to catch up with Gar.

The sun was high in the sky and as the three boys moved up the creek, the land on either side began to rise. This was casting the moving water into shadow. The yellow-haired boy moved more cautiously, occasionally leaning down to search the ground. When Gar realized he was pulling out ahead of the other two, he slowed. The Bronco was easy to track, the additional weight of Nalin's body pushing his moccasins deeper into the soft loam.

The man's stride became longer as he picked up speed. "We must move faster," the Kid said. John Daisy said, "This bik'endiihi moves very fast." Gar was looking upstream but John Daisy's dark eyes were on Shonto's Kid. "If he gets out too far in front he'll stop and abuse the girl or kill her! If we can catch him and make him think we are many, he may abandon her and run."

Gar spoke, "He will be very dangerous. He is big and has many scars of many battles!"

John Daisy said in a low growl, "The winter bear can be brought down by three hungry wolves." He turned and moved quickly up the stream. The Kid looked across the stream. That side wasn't as steep now.

"I'll take the other side," the Kid said, splashing across. "You stay with John Daisy," he called to Gar.

"This one takes no orders from a white child." Gar snorted.

Ugashe' ignored him. The white boy ran a clumsy route, moving as quickly as the rocks and the stream would let him. His eyes were riveted to the ground, searching for any sign that the outlaw had come across and changed directions. In quick glances he could see John Daisy up ahead on the other side. He was having the same trouble with footing the Kid was having. The yellow-haired boy was thinking if the man was not alone, and they ran into a war party, there would be four easy scalps for the price of one.

On they raced. The minutes and tens of minutes went by and the ground on the Kid's side of the creek began to rise. It was moving on a gradual incline until it was threatening to become a sheer cliff. There was a canyon ahead. The ground on John Daisy's side rose also but there was a passable area alongside the stream.

The Kid ran higher, forced upward along the rising edge of the cliff. Soon his feet were racing several yards above John Daisy's head. The stream had widened, and John Daisy was thirty long paces to his left. All three of the boys knew this area. They had hunted and explored it. They knew that John Daisy and Gar's side of the creek would open wider into a flood plain, this bordered by sheer walls.

The Kid at his elevation would soon be able to see a good distance down the canyon. The footing smoothed out on his side, and he began to make better time, pulling ahead of the other two. As he came over a knoll, he spotted the renegade moving across the flats, Nalin's bare rump slung over his shoulder.

He called like a dove.

John Daisy pulled up, looking upward toward him. Using broad motions, the Kid signaled how far ahead the renegade was. He motioned he would circle out in front and get ahead of the man. Even though the man was fully grown, the Kid was very quick and would have no trouble passing him. The only trouble would be doing it silently.

Ugashe' turned and raced along the top. The ground was flatter now and the footing more even. There was no sound but the whisper of the long grass against the soft leather of the white boy's knee-high moccasins. He ran like a deer, his long blond hair streaming behind. One hand was on the handle of the long, razor-sharp skinning knife that had once belonged to Shonto Page.

The sun had moved in the sky and was warm. There was no wind. The blood ran through the boy's veins and despite the danger ahead he found himself exhilarated by the chase. He also was aware the girl's life depended on him getting in front without being seen.

The Kid knew the area ahead. He knew the creek bed below him would finally peter out into a jumble of high cliffs and boulders. It was here that the Bronco would have to abandon the creek and go to high ground. He would need to come to the Kid's side. It was at that point the Kid would have to be waiting, with the man and his burden halfway up the canyon wall and John Daisy and Gar at his back. The most dangerous moment would be the moment the Bronco knew they were there. He might simply cut Nalin's throat and run for it.

The Kid knew that now he was past the Bronco. He moved as silently and as quickly as he could for another two hundred yards. He finally reached the spot he was sure the Bronco would choose to climb out. He found a vantage point that gave him a clear view but also offered shelter. This was where they would make their stand. John Daisy and Gar below, him above. He squatted on his heels, his chest heaving. If the Bronco chose the easiest place to climb out, he would climb up directly toward the Kid.

He didn't have long to wait. Lying flat, with only the top of his head and his eyes showing but not silhouetted, he watched the Bronco coming. The renegade came into view carrying Nalin. The girl was still out cold. The man moved easily but cautiously. For the first time the Kid realized just how big and powerful the man was. He carried Nalin like a boy would carry a rabbit.

The man reached the spot below and realized that he would have to climb. He dumped Nalin unceremoniously onto the ground. Reaching into his pack he pulled a length of rawhide rope and trussed the girl expertly. She began to awaken. The Kid slid backward, out of sight. He held his breath. He could hear Nalin moaning.

Suddenly, he heard Gar and John Daisy race into view. The Kid stood as the outlaw swung to face them. Gar let out a scream of anger and the two boys raced recklessly toward the man. In one move the Bronco reached down and grabbed a fist full of Nalin's hair. He dragged her to her feet and held her out in front of him.

Now she was conscious and stood weakly, her knees weak and her eyes closed. The man put a knife to her throat and the two boys skidded to a halt about twenty yards away. Gar started forward but John Daisy put a hand to his arm, holding him back.

With the Bronco's attention on the two boys, the Kid moved forward. Looking down from above he was again struck by how large the man was, his body crisscrossed by scars. Compared to the two boys, he was huge. It was like two small dogs holding a lion at bay.

The Bronco's eyes moved past the two boys, looking for the other warriors he was sure would be following. In a deadly moment he realized the boys were alone. An evil grin came over his face. He viciously threw Nalin to the ground and she cried out in pain. He started toward the boys.

With a sudden cry, Gar rushed forward, his knife held high. From above, the Kid admired the boy's bravery. It was stupid, but brave. The Bronco easily slipped the boy's charge and slashed at Gar as the boy stumbled by. The knife blade sliced across Gar's cheek, cutting deep to the bone and teeth. The blood gushed down the boy's chest. Gar stumbled back, staring in amazement at his blood-covered hand. The Bronco hit him in the temple with the butt end of his knife and Gar dropped like a stone.

The big man now turned to John Daisy with a broad smile. Holding the bloody knife out front the man took a step forward. John Daisy stood empty handed, but he held his ground. The Bronco was pleased at this and laughed.

Nalin lay to the side moaning, trying to sit up. John Daisy pulled her dress from his belt and casually tossed it to her. She grabbed it, struggling to pull it in front of her to cover her nakedness. John Daisy reached to his moccasin and pulled the bone handled knife that had belonged to his father. The Bronco laughed again and started forward. John Daisy began to move side to side, and the white boy began to work his way down the canyon wall, moving as silently as possible from boulder to boulder.

John Daisy moved back and forth, trying to keep the Bronco's back to Ugashe'. The Bronco evidently sensed that this one was not as rash as the first and moved more cautiously. Even a small dog has sharp teeth.

The Bronco began to talk to John Daisy. "Little woman," he said, calling to the boy. "Little woman, come and dance with

24

me." He smiled broadly. "Today you die, little woman."

John Daisy began to yip at the man, like a coyote. The smile left the outlaw's face and he lunged, his knife slicing through the air. John Daisy danced backwards, then slashed at the Bronco's outstretched arm. The man jerked back just in time to avoid a serious gash. John Daisy had learned his lessons well. When fighting with the knife, you cut the closest thing to you. A man with forearms slashed to the bone will not hold his knife long. They circled again. Ugashe' was halfway down.

Nalin had gotten her dress in front of her and was trying to untie her hands with her teeth. She made small mewing noises as she struggled. The Kid was now twenty feet above the two circling men. He found a rock the size of a melon and waited for the Bronco to come beneath him.

John Daisy could see his white brother and tried to lure the big man into the spot beneath his waiting shik'isn. He thrust the knife at the outlaw trying to force him to take a step backward, but instead, the Bronco suddenly dropped to the ground. Swinging his feet, he kicked John Daisy's forward leg out from beneath him. John Daisy landed heavily on his back! The Bronco scrambled to his feet. His knife came up, ready to pin the boy to the earth. The Kid launched the rock with both hands.

The rock seemed to float end over end down through the sunlight. To the Kid it seemed that the rock sailed for minutes. It caught the man on the point of his shoulder and knocked him sideways. His knife flew from his numbed hand, and he stumbled forward, almost running, like someone out of balance running downhill. He fell directly onto John Daisy. Nalin screamed!

Ugashe' made the bottom of the cliff in two jumps and landed heavily, rolling to his feet. He started toward the two men. John Daisy was struggling violently and finally managed to push the man off of him. In the center of the man's chest, only the bone handle of John Daisy's knife was visible. The man was stone dead.

John Daisy struggled to his feet, covered with the man's blood. He looked at the Kid, then to Nalin, then back to the dead man. He threw his head back and howled like a wolf.

The Kid walked over to where Gar was struggling to sit up. His eyes were still slightly unfocused. The Kid turned to Nalin and quickly sliced through the leather thongs that bound her. Her dark eyes flashed at him, defiantly. She held the dress in front to cover herself.

The Kid said in English, "Ma'am, this wouldn't happen if you were ugly."

Nalin didn't know what he was saying.

"If she were ugly, he would have just killed her," John Daisy said.

"Yeah," the Kid said. "There is that."

Nalin jerked her dress on and turned and began running back to the camp.

6

John Daisy knew where to find Ochocama in the red rock canyons. Ochocama's rancheria was small in number and had learned to move easily and carefully. They still roamed free because they lived off the land. Ochocama forbid them what came most naturally, which was raiding and stealing. The Mexicans were fair game, but he left the whites alone.

But the Kid had heard the white soldiers talking at the poker table and they said things were about to change. Crook's superiors thought he was too soft on the Apaches. The Kid thought it only a matter of time before the Army would move on Ochacama. The dance business would only make it worse.

Manuelito and the other White Mountain scouts, who had been severely loyal to Crook, and who had even been used to hunt down their own relatives, found some humor and some pride in knowing that there was one band of Dinee still free.

It was two days of travel from Stolvig's to the canyon area. John Daisy and the Kid camped the first night at the round lake. It was a natural seep, high in the pines, surrounded by thick forest. The shoreline was so thick with willows that the water was almost impossible to get to without ending up waist deep in mud and thick weeds.

They made their camp away from the water on a ridge. They built a small, sheltered fire. They were in their bedrolls before the last of the light was out of the sky. When the first light hit the tops of the trees, they were up and moving. Breakfast was jerky and a chunk of hard unleavened bread. The Kid rode a big buckskin. It reminded him of Shonto Page's old horse. His traveling gear was also like Shonto's. And like Shonto, he carried two pistols when riding, one on his hip with a leather loop over the hammer. He had Shonto's old Walker Colt in a belly holster. Because of the size of the pistol, the holster was made special and sat just left of his belt buckle sideways on his belt. Riding easy, his hands on the horn, he could lift it out easily.

His rifle was hooked in under his left leg. It was protected by a beaded and fringed leather sheath. His bedroll was lashed behind him, on the saddle. Saddlebags carried his worldly possessions.

The Kid couldn't stay in one place for very long. He had trailed behind Shonto Page for seven years and once he and John Daisy were old enough, they had left the rancheria to roam far and wide. They wrangled wild horses and sold them to the Army. They trapped fur-bearing animals and sold the fur, even though this bored John Daisy to tears. Another sure money maker was the Kid's skill with cards. He had been taught early by Shonto Page and was better than most.

Why John Daisy tagged along was no mystery. He didn't have any choice. Ugashe' was gonna go anyway, and the alternative was to waste away on the reservation or hide in the mountains with Ochocama. John Daisy wasn't much of a hider, and the thought of being restricted to the reservation was repugnant.

John Daisy gave the appaloosa her head and she set a good pace, working through the trees. The Kid followed with just a vague idea of where they were headed. By mid-morning they were skirting the high grassy meadows.

The Kid could tell that his young Indian friend was troubled by what the Army scout, Manuelito, had told him. Apparently, Noch-ay-del-Klinne's vision was the talk of the reservation. Noch-ay-del-Klinne had been told by the spirits in his vision that the People would soon be free of the white man's yoke. He had been told that their ancestors would rise and help the People chase the white man from their lands. Noch-ay-del-Klinne had resurrected the Shadow Dances. And his two main disciples were the girl, Nalin, and their old childhood friend, Gar.

Riding down a gradual slope, their pony's legs swishing through the high meadow tobosa grass, John Daisy mused about the most troubling thing the Army scout had told him. Gar had taken to wearing a special buckskin shirt during the ceremonial dances. A shirt with mystic signs beaded into it and rubbed with the ash of the cottonwoods until the shirt shined white in the moonlight. The spirit shirts had not been used for many years. The old ones that believed in them said they were impenetrable. The magic could stop lance or arrow or bullet. This bothered John Daisy because he no longer believed in this kind of magic. Hadn't believed it for a long time.

When Ugashe' came to live in his lodge the white child had shown him that there were two worlds and now John Daisy could see and understand more than many others. He could not believe in magic that would stem the tide of white soldiers. He could not believe in magic shirts whose owners were no longer alive to testify to their powers. But John Daisy knew that the young men on the reservation were ready to believe about anything that promised a return to the old ways. John Daisy knew that the spirit shirt was a troubling thing. And John Daisy was troubled for Nalin. Manuelito had said that the girl's stature had grown almost as powerful as Noch-ay-del-Klinne's. John Daisy had always known the girl to be very logical in thought and practical in action. For her to become a leader of this Shadow Dance movement was astounding to the young man.

The day had passed with the steady and rhythmic gait of the two horses. It was enough to lull a man to sleep. Suddenly John Daisy reined the appaloosa to a halt. The Kid smelled it at the same time. Wood smoke. They carefully reined their ponies into the trees. The wind was moving softly from the southwest. This meant the smoke originated from deeper in the pine forest. Leaning low over the saddle to avoid the tree limbs, the Kid urged his horse wide and deeper into the forest. The Walker Colt was automatically in his hand. John Daisy pulled his rifle from its scabbard and set it easily across the saddle. He swung the appaloosa out in the other direction and urged the mare forward.

The ground was covered with a million years of pine needles, but the going wasn't that easy. Crystallized volcanic rock had pushed up through the loam and the ponies had to pick their way carefully around these obstacles. The two riders drifted further into the trees until barely visible to one another. The Kid kept his eyes forward, not searching, but relaxed. The easiest thing to see in a forest was movement. Shonto had taught him that you could be staring at a still man and never see him, but a tree-colored lizard could be seen at fifty yards if it were moving.

When the Kid glanced over again at John Daisy, the Indian was out of sight. The Kid kept his horse at the easy pace. The pony stepped softly on the forest floor. Ahead of him he heard a horse blow. He pulled the pony to a halt. He sat still, holding his pony up tight. Several yards ahead, the horse blew again and tossed its head. The Kid eased out of the saddle and holding the pony by the bridle, moved slowly forward. Through the trees he could make out a camp. He slid down and snubbed his pony to a tree branch and replaced the Walker Colt in its holster. He eased the Winchester out of the scabbard. He started forward again, his moccasined feet whispering on the pine needles. He didn't come directly at the camp. It appeared to be a one-man camp and the man wasn't home. A faint wisp of smoke trickled from a campfire that held coals and a coffeepot. A bedroll was off to the side.

A haunch of venison hung from a limb on a nearby tree. High enough for varmints not to get it. There were two animals. A horse and a pack mule. The pack mule's load lay beside the bedroll. There was a slight movement on the other side, then John Daisy, rifle up, moved into the clearing. The Kid stepped forward. "Nobody home," he stated.

"Hell there ain't!" said a voice above him. The Kid looked up into the barrel of a fifty caliber Henry. Behind the rifle was the bewhiskered and grinning old face of Delnorte.

"I God," he growled, then spit a stream of tobacco juice. "You two pups make more noise than a herd of bufflers!"

7

Delnorte swung down, one-handed, out of that tree. He fixed John Daisy with a baleful look. "Your daddy would've skinned ye," he said. He turned and pinned the Kid with the same eye. "Shonto, too! You young'ns been taught that there's more ways to look than just left and right."

John Daisy laughed. "I had you, old man, I was waitin' on the white child."

"Wait and be damned." the Kid said sourly.

"Got coffee on," Delnorte said, moving an arm to the fire. He turned, a twinkling in his eye. "Put it on when I heard ye comin' 'bout an hour ago." Sure enough, two tin cups were set up on a log. The Kid squatted down cross-legged and snatched one up. He reached for the pot.

"Hot now," Delnorte warned.

The Kid gingerly lifted the pot and poured a cup. He left John Daisy's empty, him not being partial to it. He knew that Delnorte knew this but was only making his point. He was chagrinned to have been caught off guard. He looked over at the old man, regaining his humor. It was good to see him. It had been over a year. Delnorte was officially John Daisy's uncle, having ridden into the territory twenty years ago when white men were damn scarce, and Mexicans only ventured out in groups of fifty or more. Delnorte had hunted and trapped the entire territory from the Sierra Madres to the Colorado, mostly alone, but sometimes with a partner. At one time his partner had been Shonto Page, long before Shonto Page had taken the Kid to raise. Sometimes a man can be alone only so long. Sometimes a man reaches a point in his life, when he looks at himself and it's not enough, then he needs more. Needs someone to share the experiences with. Not like a partner. Not like a good friend. More like sharing the soul and the heart. Delnorte had needed a wife.

He had ridden four days to the southwest and after finding the Mexican settlement that suited his designs, he emptied a corral of mustangs and drove them through the dark, all night and all day, not sleeping. Kept them moving until two days later he found a canyon to hold them. He was in the heart of Apacheria but he slept fitfully. When he awoke, he drove the herd to Ochocama's rancheria.

Ochocama knew this white man. Had known him for years. Had given him safety as a sound man and a shrewd swapper. Now this white man rode into the heart of the largest rancheria driving fifteen ponies ahead of him. He was a rich man. He could have any eligible woman that would have him back.

Delnorte herded the ponies to Ochocama's lodge and kept them bunched until the boy children, the ishkiin, secured them in a mesquite pole corral. Delnorte then made an offer for Ochocama's eldest daughter, Juh. As the years would prove,

Delnorte had not only selected a good woman, but secured his stature in the territory.

Ordinarily, Delnorte was not a man of many words, so the Kid wasn't surprised that the old man settled himself on the ground and dug his chaw out of his cheek and flung it away. He then pulled his pipe and started packing it, all without a word. It was hard to determine how old Delnorte was. Although his body was thinning with age, he was still wiry and strong. He sported a full beard which it had taken Juh years to grow accustomed to. His hair was long and white, and his face was seamed with the lines of his years.

John Daisy kicked a mound of pine needles, then sat quietly on them, staring out into the forest. The Kid waited patiently. After some time, he asked, "What brings you up this high?" Delnorte ordinarily operated a way station on the Cherry Road. A place for travelers to stop between Prescott and Fort Verde. It was there the Kid and John Daisy had the run in with Long Bedeaux and his gang the year before. The Kid sported a crease in his skull and John Daisy carried scar tissue at the top of his shoulder. Bedeaux and all of his had six feet of dirt.

Delnorte took a long drag on his pipe and blew a stream of smoke. "Venison," he said. "Ol' woman of mine is tired of beef and beans. And I sometimes get tired of being cooped up."

"Juh is Dinee." John Daisy agreed. "She needs venison."

Delnorte pointed his pipe stem at John Daisy. "Yer aunt has done jest fine on beef and beans. Just need a change once a while." He grinned at the Kid. "Trouble is, we're both gettin' older and we don't process them beans like we use'ta. Wintertime, especially. We close up that house and get to fart'n

34

them frijoles, it gets downright dangerous in there."

"Fact is," Delnorte continued, "besides fittin' Juh's tooth for deer meat, I'm glad I run into you boys." He nodded at the Kid. "Sam Perkins the driver fer the stage dropped off a message 'bout a month ago for you."

"What kind of message?"

He took another suck on his pipe, then leaned over and fooled with the embers. Finally, he cocked an eye up. "There's a woman looking for ye." He knew this would set the Kid back and he grinned when it did.

"What kind of woman?" the Kid asked.

The old man guffawed. "Perkins says she's a looker."

John Daisy was grinning, knowing that the Kid and women weren't a natural combination.

"I don't know any women," the Kid said lamely.

"Hell boy, that don't surprise me none," Delnorte said with a twinkle. "But you know this one." He leaned over and spit into the ashes. "Lucille Baldwin's lookin' for ye."

The Kid shook his head. "Don't know no Lucille Baldwin."

"Suppose not," the old man said. "But you know Miss Lucy don't ye?"

The Kid knew Miss Lucy. Every man in the territory knew Miss Lucy. The Kid had met Miss Lucy when he was a boy trailing behind Shonto Page. For the last fifteen years she'd run the Golden Bear on Whiskey Row in Prescott. After spending a few months following Shonto Page around the mountains there wasn't anything better to the young boy than sleeping in a warm tick bed. That, and eating the fixings in her kitchen as her large black cook ladled it on his plate. Miss Lucy had been at

Delnorte's station during the Bedeaux shoot out.

"Word is, that if I was to run into you, Miss Lucy wants you to come to town and see her. Says she needs yer help."

"Nothing more?"

Delnorte shook his head. "All Perkins knew."

The Kid looked to John Daisy. John Daisy shrugged, "Go ahead."

"You going on to Ochocama's?"

John Daisy nodded. Delnorte looked at the young Indian sharply.

"You headin' up to the rancheria?"

"We hear Noch-ay-del-Klinne is headed up there," he said.

Delnorte shook his head. "I smell a bad wind blowin'. This dance business ain't gonna come to no good end."

"You know about that?"

The old man nodded. "Juh's people stop by once in a while. Soldier boys too. The word is that ol' Crook has been replaced by a guy named Carr. Hard man from what I hear. Not as smart as Crook."

John Daisy shrugged. "The people want hope."

"Hope is one thing, suicide is another." Delnorte knocked his pipe against his leg. "Nothin' but damned foolishness," he said, squinting an eye at John Daisy. "Damn near had to knock yer aunt in the head to keep her out of it."

John Daisy stood up. "My grandfather will need me."

"Ain't no doubt," Delnort said. He looked to the Kid. "You goin' with him?"

The Kid looked to John Daisy. He shook his head. "Reckon I'll head to Miss Lucy's and get her taken care of, then I'll head up there."

36

Delnorte said to John Daisy, "Ain't Noch-ay-del-Klinne that's stirrin' all this up. Gar's got all them young bucks riled up. Noch-ay-del-Klinne's gal Nalin is all caught up in it too." He stood up. "When them blue-bellies show up, and with Carr in charge, and you damn well know that they will, you get yer grandfather outa there. Get him down to the Madres."

John Daisy walked over to his appaloosa and swung up. The Kid followed behind. The Kid mounted, then nudged his pony over by Delnorte.

Delnorte said, "Watch yerself in that white man's town, boy. There be a powerful lot of sinners down there."

"I'll watch'm," the Kid smiled. He nudged his pony and raised a hand in salute. "Watch your pretty hair, old man."

The old man waggled his pipe at the Kid. "Watch yorn, boy."

He pointed the pipe stem at the retreating John Daisy. "And keep an eye on his'n too."

8

Prescott was nestled in the crook and valley of the high mountains. Surrounded by tall pines and juniper, the town had blossomed with the lure of gold in the high hills and the jingle of hard U.S. currency in the pockets of blue-coat soldiers. The high end of the Cherry Road stretched in from the east, crossing the wide, endless, high desert plains. With the Apaches on the reservation at San Carlos, the road was now widely traveled.

It was two days after the chance meeting with Delnorte when John Daisy and the Kid parted at the high end of the Cherry Road. The Kid rode west. John Daisy headed east to the high red rock canyons. The Kid rode easy in the saddle, smoking an occasional cigarette. He knew this territory. He knew it well. He had learned the lay of the grass and the rambling curves of the washes while following behind Shonto Page's big buckskin stud.

He mused on the notion that many years ago he had been following one of the Territories' most celebrated gunmen into Prescott to visit a gal. Now he rode the same road to see the very same woman. The gunman was long gone, the woman had grown older, the Kid had grown to manhood and the town had gotten bigger, no longer the mud road and ramshackle buildings clustered together in the crooked valley. But now, a muscled and tempered town, bustling with activity and new stores and homes. Buildings that housed new hopes and dreams, springing up and sprawling across the hills and winding slopes

The Kid walked his pony down the long grade, enjoying the morning sunlight in the crisp, bright air. Moving through the streets he noted streetlamps placed systematically in places they had not been before. The main streets were busy with people. People afoot, people on horseback and people in carts and wagons. The Kid hadn't seen so many people in one place since Santa Fe. As he progressed into the heart of the town, he became aware of the stares he was receiving. At first mystified and uncomfortable, he suddenly realized that it was his dress that drew the looks. He noted the men around him and they were mostly fitted in dark broadcloth jackets and trousers, or shapeless canvass pants and collarless cotton shirts. He, on the other hand, wore a buckskin shirt with most of the fringe pulled, and cloth trousers tucked into knee high, leather moccasins. He wore a flat brimmed leather hat with a thin, leather strap under his chin. His hair was long and blond, burned almost white by the sun. He carried his Walker in the belly holster and the Colt on his leg. He had to smile to himself. He looked like a long-tooth wolf come to a hen house party. He stopped at a boy playing with a tin can in the dust. The boy stepped back two steps and just stared at him, eyes wide.

The Kid laughed softly. "I ain't gonna eat you boy, I just need to find my animal a bait of grain. Where's the closest livery?"

The boy stood wide-eyed, then slowly raised an arm and

pointed down the street. The Kid smiled and touched his hat. "Much obliged."

He nudged his pony on and, after a block, looked back. The boy stood rooted, watching him. He found the livery and paid the man for a day and began to strip the animal down. The livery man offered but the Kid declined. Shonto had taught him that a man always takes care of two things himself. His mount and his guns.

The Kid piled his saddle and his other truck in a corner where the stable man could keep an eye on it. He pulled off the belly holster and stashed it in his bedroll. He unloaded the Winchester and wiped it off, running a soft cloth in the breech. He sheathed the rifle in the beaded case that had been handcrafted by the talented fingers of old Nino. He slung his possible bag over his shoulder and headed out of the gloomy shade of the livery into the bright street.

In the days when Prescott was just another stop in the road, the Golden Bear Saloon was the largest building in town. Not just the largest but the most important. The center of all social activity. A man could not only find drink and comfort there, he could also, on occasion, watch a fair trial and a true hanging.

Before the Kid's time, when Shonto Page was new to this country and Delnorte was about the only white man in the mountains, when the great war between north and south had ended and victory was celebrated by death and devastation by both, the territory had been flooded by homeless, gaunt eyed men searching for a new life. Then the Golden Bear Saloon had been owned and run by a huge, loud, good-hearted woman by the name of Flora.

Flora had made the Golden Bear a home to the wandering man where he could find comfort with a woman or with a bottle, for about the same price. Flora catered to the miners and trappers and the occasional soldier. She catered to Mexicans and Californios and to men on either side of the law. In other words, Flora had half the human race as prospective clients. She had two rules. You don't spit tobacco juice on the girls, and you don't discharge a firearm inside the bar. The sign said, *Inside the bar!* She was asked why just inside the bar, why not in the rest of the building. She laughed and she said that it paid damn good money to let a man discharge his weapon upstairs.

She could be a hard woman, not suffering any insult from anyone. She cold-cocked more than one troublemaker and manhandled him to the street, tossing him into the dirt. But she was the easiest mark in town. Any hard luck story could get a meal. Not a drink, but a meal. She outfitted more than one down on his luck miner and never saw the return.

It was to Flora that Shonto Page had brought the young, skinny and badly abused Lucy Baldwin. Shonto had come across her in the mountains, the bought and paid-for property of a buffalo man. The girl was about twelve years old, and the buffalo man had used her badly. When Shonto had brought her from the mountains, the buffalo man was dead in the mountains, suffering an overdose of Shonto's skinning knife. The girl clung to him.

Not having any experience with girl children, Shonto took her to the only place in the Territory that he knew she would be treated decently. He brought her to the Golden Bear. Miss Lucy grew up at the Golden Bear, and when Flora's great old heart finally gave out, the Golden Bear became hers.

Miss Lucy expanded it as the Territory grew. When gold fever raged because of the fist sized nuggets found at Antelope Springs, she diversified into the gambling business. Her soiled doves were still there, but Miss Lucy, sniffing the winds of change, began making that part of the business more discreet. As the town grew and became more of a community with families and schools, Miss Lucy had the innate good sense not to challenge the moral fiber of the burgeoning female population. The building itself sat smack in what had become a string of saloons that had blossomed around it. A famous stretch of ground, it was now the only place in the Territory that a man could be tossed out of a saloon several times and still find new avenues to conquer before daylight. It was called Whiskey Row. Simple and to the point.

In the years that Miss Lucy had the Golden Bear she became more than just the saloon girl or the whore house madam. She became an intricate part of the town. She was always discreet, but her money always chose the right cause. She always knew which sheriff to put her money behind. She was the first to donate to the orphans' home. The first to give to the local church charity. The first to contribute to the mayoral campaign. Of course, none could be given in her name or the name of the Golden Bear. An anonymous donor. A benevolent benefactor. But everyone from the local pastor to the lowest constable knew where the dollars originated.

Miss Lucy's girls were clean and regularly checked by old Doc Morgan. The constable routinely patrolled her place at night and was ready to evict any troublesome interloper. Of course, he benefited with wonderful birthdays and Christmases and an occasional surprise in between. And, once, when a newcomer brought forth an ingenious plan for increasing township revenues by taxing the saloons, he was unanimously defeated in the next election. Miss Lucy ran a tight ship.

The Kid walked the hollow-sounding wooden boardwalk, amazed at how the town had grown in the short time since he had been through. He walked easily, his fringed and beaded rifle sheath carried carelessly across the back of his neck. He watched with pleasure as the ladies of the town hurried about their business, dressed in full, petticoated skirts. It was a hot day, and he couldn't understand how they could stand it. Apache women would be dressed in easy-moving and spacious dresses. It appeared to him that a Dinee woman dressed for comfort. A white woman dressed for show.

The Kid finally found himself standing across the street from the Golden Bear. It hadn't changed much outside, except for the wooden boardwalk around it. The Kid stepped out into the street and walked across. He stepped up on the walk and stopped just outside the opened batwing doors. On the street the light was bright, inside the building it was dark. He stared into the dark a few moments, letting his eyes adjust. When he finally went in, it was at a slight angle. Nothing noticeable to anyone inside. He moved to the side and waited for his eyes to finish their adjustment.

9

The pungent odors of smoke, whiskey, and beer assailed his nostrils. It was not unpleasant but living in the clean wind of the mountains made the sense of smell sensitive to civilization. Riding with Shonto he had learned that Shonto had always been very fastidious with his guns, his horse and his body. At first the Kid thought it unusual for a man to bathe so often but it was a habit of Shonto's that the Kid had picked up.

The Kid took his time looking around. The Golden Bear had two stories and the ground floor was huge with a long wooden bar running the length of one wall. The rest of the room was filled with tables and chairs designed for card players. The back of the room boasted a huge, colorful upright roulette wheel that stood at least eight feet tall. Though it was early in the day, the place was more than half filled. The Kid figured it must be Saturday, or at least payday, as most of the men in the room were soldiers. The rest carried the roughhewn look of men that worked a bone-hard life with their hands: miners or farmers, cowmen or mule skinners.

Immediately to the Kid's left was a wall full of pegs and on the pegs, there dangled an assortment of pistol belts. Under each peg was a painted number. Across the walnut bar a man stood, his substantial girth wrapped in a clean white apron. His hair was dark and slicked back, straight away from his forehead. He had a huge moustache that was greased and pointed on the ends. He had a smile and friendly eyes. He was looking at the Kid, waiting. The Kid smiled, then nodded to the peg board.

"This something new?"

The bartender shook his head, still smiling. "Not new to me, friend. Miss Lucy's rules. If you come in here, you can do so without fear of getting shot in the back. We check all firearms."

Surrendering his pistol was not to the Kid's liking, and while he was making up his mind, the bartender's eyes shifted across the room and lit on a big, bearded man. The man held a walking stick as long as his arm and as thick as his wrist, which was considerable. The Kid recognized him. Franz had been Miss Lucy's bouncer for many years. The big man was standing toward the back, watching a poker game between some bluebellies and a farmer. The Kid turned his eyes back to the bartender and the bartender was still watching him, still smiling, his eyes a little more cautious. The Kid smiled again.

"As long as Old Franz is on the job, I suppose I'll be safe," he said, unbuckling his belt. He handed it to the bartender. The bartender took the belt with a chuckle and hung it on a peg. He handed the Kid a round wooden poker chip with a number on it that coincided with the peg number.

"Bring this back when you're ready to leave," he said.

The Kid started to move down the bar, but the bartender raised a hand to stop him. "I'll need that too," he said, indicating the rifle.

The Kid lay the rifle up on the bar and unfastened the end of the sheath. He slid the Winchester out until the breech was exposed. He levered it and showed the empty chamber to the man. "Empty," he said. He levered it several more times to show there was nothing in the weapon. He looked at the bartender with cool, pale eyes. "I ain't partial to leavin' this just layin around somewhere."

The bartender nodded. "Keep it cased and it'll be okay." He smiled at the Kid. "I don't recall seein' you around here. You sure you are old enough to drink?"

"Yeah, I'm old enough, but I don't drink much anyhow."

"Don't believe I've seen you before. You new around here?"

"Been a while," the Kid admitted.

"Well, young fella, you find yourself a comfortable spot and the first beer is on Miss Lucy. It's her policy to make all newcomers welcome."

"Obliged," the Kid returned. He moved left to the end of the bar where it curved around. This put the door to his right and the rest of the room in front of him. He laid the sheathed Winchester up on the bar and hooked a moccasined foot on the brass footrest. The bartender brought him a foaming glass of beer. He wiped the bar in front of the Kid.

"Name's Robert Erven," he offered. "Most call me Bobby."

"Howdy," the Kid said, tasting the beer. He looked at it in surprise.

The bartender was grinning. "This is cold," the Kid said in amazement.

"Only cold beer in the Territory."

"How do you do that?" the Kid asked, taking another swallow.

"Man came to town about six months ago and started up an ice-house. Miss Lucy was one of his first customers. Costs her a lot but she don't pass it on. Man built her some kinda double-walled box to put the ice in and we put the beer barrels right on top." He wiped a spot on the bar. "It's a wonderment to folks out here but I'm from Chicago, so I didn't think much about it."

"Cold beer in the summertime," the Kid said, shaking his head.

"What's your name?" the bartender asked.

The Kid hesitated.

"None of my business if you don't want to tell me."

The Kid smiled. "You're right. You're not from around here. Most people aren't that up front. They think it's unfriendly. Figure if someone wants you to know, they'll tell you."

Bobby smiled. "I appreciate the advice. But, what if you and me was to be friends, I'd have to call you something."

The Kid took another drink. "Well, Bobby. . . one side of the family calls me 'Ugashe'."

Bobby cocked his head. "Never heard that name before."

"Dinee for *get*. Like *get* the hell outa here."

"Dinee?"

"Apache."

"You pullin' my leg?"

"No sir!"

"So that's what they call you?"

"The old man that raised me just called me Kid so that's what most folks call me."

"Kid, huh?" He picked up the Kid's empty glass and raised an eyebrow.

The Kid nodded and the man stepped over and tapped another. He set it in front on the bar.

"Ten cents," he said.

The Kid dug out the money, "Expensive beer!"

Bobby shook his head, "Not in Chicago. And remember it's the only cold beer in the territory." He moved down the bar and deposited the money. A couple of other men at the bar needed refills and he moved down and took care of them. In a few moments he came back to where the Kid stood.

"Knew a fighter on the south side named Kid Bordello. Bordello's a whore house, you know."

The Kid shook his head.

"French," Bobby explained. "Poor bastard got his bell rung too many times, ended up swabbing spittoons."

"Hard way to make a livin,'" the Kid agreed. "Miss Lucy upstairs?"

The bartender stopped and his eyes turned cool. "Miss Lucy don't see anyone. Especially in the daytime. You want a girl? You talk to Miss Molly, Miss Molly will fix you up with one of the girls." Bobby put a hand out and patted him on the arm. "Miss Lucy's too damn old for a buck like you anyway." A man down the bar signaled with an empty glass and Bobby turned away. He walked down to the other end of the long bar.

The Kid sipped on his beer and studied the room. Pretty quiet day. Just the murmur of voices of men whiling away a morning playing cards. The Kid noticed that Franz was still watching the same table of players. What was unusual was that Franz was fixated on the farmer at the table with the soldiers. The farmer was a tall, rangy looking raw-boned fellow. He looked drunk and he didn't look like he was having fun.

The Kid had noticed him when he first came in. He also noticed a smaller version of the guy sitting at a table by himself, his head on his arms. It was when the farmer slammed his cards onto the table, loosing a string of curse words at one of the soldiers when the sleeper raised his head. The two wore the same faded overalls and patched shirts and bore a striking resemblance to each other. They both had hair like straw, freckles and a thin inbred look in their eyes.

Franz moved closer to the older farmer. The soldier had also won the deal and without paying attention to the farmer's tirade, shuffled and dealt out a new hand. The Kid drank some more beer.

The farmer grabbed a fistful of cards from the table and threw them at the soldier. He shoved himself back and threw his half-filled beer mug against the far wall. Franz reached down and grasped the guy by the back of his shirt. He jerked the man to his feet. The soldiers all scrambled backwards.

The farmer's voice was shrill and harsh. "That goddam Yankee's cheatin' me!"

10

Franz jerked him up on his tiptoes, growling "You are done, boy. Get outa here and don't come back."

"But they been cheating me." The guy whined loudly.

"I've been watching the whole time," Franz said in his Teutonic growl. "No one is cheating you. You are just a lousy poker player."

Franz started to haul the farmer out when the younger version came to his feet and made two quick steps toward them. In his hand was a pocket derringer. Quick as a snake he thrust it up under Franz's jowl. Franz froze. The boy thumbed the hammer back, the sound large in the suddenly quiet room. The elder farmer jerked himself free of Franz's grip.

He was grinning now. "Guess we got a whole new situation."

The Kid set his beer mug down and slid his hand up in the leather sheath of the rifle case and grasped the handle, his finger finding the trigger. He stepped away from the bar. The younger of the yokels was grinning broadly, his yellowed horse teeth gleaming in the near dark.

The elder took a step forward and hit the baby-faced soldier in the nose as hard as he could. The soldier went backward, blood gushing. Franz remained frozen, his eyes on big brother waiting for him to make a mistake. From across the room the Kid could see the control that the big man was exerting, his back erect, a muscle tic in his cheek.

Little brother was smiling now, "Yessir, we got us a new situation now, don't we Farley?"

"Different than you figure," the Kid said in an even voice. He swung the sheathed barrel of the rifle around on the top of the bar till it was pointed dead at big brother's chest. To emphasize his point, he thumbed the hammer back. Every head except Franz's swiveled to him. The big gangly farmer's eyes were wide. He stared at the tall, slender, long-haired, rough-looking young man with the pale eyes that stood before him.

The Kid's eyes were locked on him. They didn't waver. The Kid, in an even voice, said, "What I've got here is a 44/40 with a soft lead slug. I've cut a cross into it. What that cross means is that when it hits you, it will make an entrance hole the size of your thumbnail and then passing through your guts it will destroy your bone and guts and spread out inside before blowing a hole out your back the size of your palm. Be a helluva mess to clean off the wall."

Big brother's mouth slid from a grin to a lopsided, sloppy-mouthed gape. His eyes shifted from the Kid's eyes to the sheathed rifle and back again. Then he looked at the covered rifle real hard. He glanced over to little brother. Little brother was staring at the Kid.

Finally big brother spoke to the Kid. "Why you pointin' that at me? I ain't got the shooter." He pointed at junior. "He's got the shooter. Why you pointin' that thing at me?"

"I just don't like you," the Kid said.

Little brother said, "Farley, he ain't supposed to have no loaded gun in here."

Big brother thought about that. "Yeah," he said. "That gun ain't supposed to be loaded."

"Ain't supposed to be," the Kid said evenly. "And little brother there ain't supposed to have that lady's gun in his boot." The Kid grinned, but it wasn't pleasant. "Looks like we both broke the rules."

Whiskey sweat was beading up on Farley and the barrel of the pocket gun had dipped a couple of inches. Little brother looked at big brother, not sure what to do. The Kid could see big brother screwing up his courage.

From above the room, from the second floor landing a woman's voice rang out, "Hey, you, Rhubarb!" There was dead silence. "You, farm boy, look up here."

Farley raised his eyes to the landing. The Kid and every other man in the room did the same. What they saw was two, big, empty eyes of a double-barreled shotgun pointing down at Farley. Behind the shotgun was the prettiest woman the Kid had ever seen. She was dressed in a shapeless frock with an apron drawn around the middle. She had pale, translucent skin and black ringlets of hair surrounding her face. Her mouth was wide and generous, and her eyes were dark slates of gray. She held the shotgun easily, like she knew how to use it. She spoke again, her voice loud enough in the big silent room. "I've got a double load of rock salt and ground copper loaded in here and damn the price, I'm just about ready to turn it loose."

The Kid involuntarily leaned against the bar, taken aback by the vision on the landing.

She waggled the barrels at Farley. "You tell your young'n, there, to put that pop gun away and you can walk out of here. You can walk out, but not to come back. Not to come back ever!" She paused. "You understand me?"

Farley was suddenly just a bumpkin, tugging at a forelock. "Yes, ma'am," he stuttered. "Didn't mean nothin', but they was cheatin' me." He turned to little brother. "Goddam it, put that away." He turned back to the landing. "Didn't mean to cause you no trouble, ma'am."

"Get out of here," she said simply.

"Yes ma'am," he said. He turned and abruptly strode across the room and out into the daylight. Little brother was caught unawares and was left standing a moment by himself. He turned and fled. "Wait up, Farley!" he called.

There was dead silence as the two of them fled through the batwings into the lighted street, then the bartender began to laugh. The young soldiers helped their friend up and they began to grin.

"I thought I'd seen it all in Chicago," the bartender laughed. He turned to the Kid. "You've got the goddamnest set of balls I've ever seen." He turned to the room. "That rifle wasn't loaded. I seen it myself." He laughed again, shaking his head. "The boy faced them down and the goddam rifle was as empty as a whore's heart!" He stopped suddenly, realizing what had come out of his mouth. He cast a stricken look at the landing, his laugh disappearing. "Sorry miss," he stumbled. "Just a joke. No offense meant."

The woman on the landing shifted the barrels of the shotgun until they pointed at the bartender. After a long moment, she said, "None taken, Chicago." Molly Sand lifted the shotgun and set the butt on the floor, her slender delicate hand holding the barrels. "But you've got a big mouth."

"Yes ma'am," Bobby said, turning away, getting busy.

She looked down at the Kid and smiled. The smile changed her face into that of a young, fresh-faced girl. The Kid suddenly realized that this shotgun toting beauty was really only about his age. She leaned both hands against the railing and peered down at him.

"So," she said. "You are the famous Shonto Page's kid?" She laughed. "Don't be surprised, Miss Lucy described you very well." She leaned forward, peering into the room. "But I don't see your Indian friend. Miss Lucy says that when you come, you'd have your Indian friend."

The Kid picked up his rifle and laid it across his shoulder. "He's close enough," he said simply.

"Well, come on up, Kid," the girl said. "Miss Lucy's waiting for you."

As the Kid started across the room to the stairs, every man in the room was watching him. As he reached the stairs, the Chicago bartender said to a nearby soldier, "Who's Shonto Page?"

The soldier looked at him, "You ain't been out here long, have you?"

At the top of the stairs, the girl motioned for the Kid to wait there. She went through a door, then was back after a couple of minutes. She signaled him to come in. He stepped in and she closed the door behind him.

11

Several millions of years before *the ones who came before* found their way to the high desert lands, the earth had been covered by a great sea. The hard rock under those waters was rent with violent volcanic eruptions. Millions of years later the waters receded, and the wind molded the sediment and the sandstone and the limestone until all was changed.

Now, a millennium later, what was left was a special area of land where the earth, colored by the red coconino sandstone and kaibab limestone, had been thrust upward in a spectacular manner, leaving canyons and buttes and spiraling towers of unimaginable beauty. The area became the canyons of the red rock, the holy ground of the People. Through this majestic beauty ran a crisp and clean stream. Flowing through the breaks in the canyon walls, it rushed a thousand feet downward, then across the canyon and out the lower end.

John Daisy guided the big appaloosa mare into the red rock country, happy to be in this holy ground. To his heart, this was his home. He knew Ochocama was here. He moved at an easy pace, his eyes ever busy, watching everything, including the ground for sign. He knew he'd have to be alert to find any. Ochocama and his small rancheria were still roaming free because of their caution.

It was this thought that lingered in John Daisy's mind and turned his thoughts to Nalin and her father. Allowing Noch-ay-del-Klinne and his followers to visit the rancheria would be disastrous to its secrecy. He knew that Ochocama had no choice and if the shadow dancer asked, the old chief would have no choice. Ochocama and the small medicine man had always been the closest of friends. In fact, Noch-ay-del-Klinne's wife, Nalin's mother, had been a cousin to Ochocama and even though it was the general custom for a Dinee male to ignore the people of his woman, Noch-ay-del-Klinne had defied custom by continuing his close friendship with Ochocama.

Time had finally done to Ochocama what his enemies could not. His once thick and glossy hair was now sparse and gray. His powerful warrior's body was now thin and gaunt with age. His eyes were failing him, but his mind was still keen. With age had come wisdom. It was this wisdom that made his counsel important to all the others. It was this wisdom that had kept his rancheria safe and free while all others were scattered into the lands south of the white man's border, or dead, or imprisoned on the reservation.

Twenty years ago, Ochocama had been a warrior among warriors, the scourge of the Sierra Madres. The *Nakaiye'*, the Mexicans, no matter in what numbers, shuddered at his war cry. Their children were forced to good behavior by threats of his coming. Noch-ay-del-Klinne had been the diyin', the Spirit Maker. The healer, the man of peace and reason. A man of uncommon intelligence and gentleness. Both were men whose voices were sought at the council fires. Their friendship had lasted the test of the years. Over the decades, the clans had fragmented, then reformed and fragmented again, and because of this the two friends had been separated, living in different rancherias during the time of war.

The war days. The days when they had all fought the hair-face blue-coat that was called Nantan Gray Wolf, the one the whites called Crook. After he brought his blue-coat soldiers and had learned to fight the Dinee way, all things changed. Now the diyin' was caged on the reservation and the old warrior hid in the mountains.

But now, the cold winds of change had stirred the dust of the dead and while the old warrior hid silently in the red rock canyons, the little diyin' had lit the fires of hope in the People. A fire that had spread as quickly as any wind sped flame in this dry and desolate land. The old warrior meditated and prayed and awaited the arrival of his old friend, knowing that not even the combined wisdom of the Healer and the Warrior could know what lay ahead.

Ochocama knew his old friend well. He knew that Noch-ay-del-Klinne would not fan the flames of danger and destruction for his people. Not wittingly. But Ochocama also knew the depths of Noch-ay-del-Klinne faith. He knew that Noch-ay-del-Klinne believed deeply in the dances. He believed fervently in the spirits of those that came before. Ochocama was wise enough to know that sometimes a man will want to believe something so much, even a false something, that in his mind it becomes true.

It started when Noch-ay-del-Klinne went to the holy

mountain with two of his followers. He danced and sang and prayed for three days. They had fasted with no water to slake their thirst and they called upon the spirits of *those that went before*. They prayed that the spirits would show them their destiny, that the spirits would come to guide them. At the end of three days, the disciples had fallen from exhaustion and Noch-ay-del-Klinne was reeling, his strength and resolve about to its end. Then the spirits appeared. Rising like the mist from the ground. Exposed from the knees up.

"Why do you call upon us?" they asked in agitation. "Why do you disturb us?"

Noch-ay-del-Klinne fell prone to the ground, his forehead pressed to the mother earth. In a trembling voice he beseeched them for guidance. Asked them to show the way for the great Dinee people to reclaim their land and their lives and to live as they had in the past.

This brought a wail of anguish from the spirits and Noch-ay-del-Klinne almost fainted from terror. His companions writhed on the ground, their hands covering unbelieving ears. When the wailing ceased, a spirit said the "ones that have gone before could not help the ones above the ground. We cannot change what has already been done. You must go back to the people, and you will soon find the peace that you seek."

At this, the spirits faded into nothing and Noch-ay-del-Klinne fell into a stupor that lasted for many hours. When Noch-ay-del-Klinne returned to the people his story was told and retold by each of the disciples that had accompanied him. Each version was different. Within five sunsets every Dinee in the Apacheria knew some version of it. But the version that became most popular was the one Gar promoted. The spirits would come and help drive the whites from Dinee land.

Noch-ay-del-Klinne knew he was looked to as the believer. He knew he must dance and see the visions. He could not let the people down. Nalin followed him, readily. His greatest disciple was Gar. Gar espoused the belief in the magic of the ghost shirts. He believed once the people moved as one against the whites their power and superiority would be revived. But, despite Gar's urging, Noch-ay-del-Klinne would do no more. Noch-ay-del-Klinne wouldn't move against the white eyes. This would have to be the action of others. It was these others, such as Gar, that brought the fear to Ochocama's heart.

12

John Daisy guided the sure-footed mare along the high trail, hugging the canyon walls as he made his way through the switchbacks and down into the valley. It was midafternoon when he stopped the appaloosa and slid from her back. With the toe of his long moccasined boot he examined horse droppings he had found on the rocky ground. Breaking them open he could tell two things. They were less than a day old and the animal that had left them behind recently came from the desert valley. Probably the reservation. The dung held grama grass and corn. Grama grass from traveling, corn from the reservation. Once he found the first sign, he found much more. They had done well to cover their passing, but that many people had to leave at least some sign. There had been many, riding and walking from the reservation area to Ochocama's rancheria.

John Daisy slid back upon the big animal. The shadow dance, he thought. They are all coming to the shadow dance. He gazed north toward the canyons. He searched for movement. He knew where they were, and he knew there were many of them. Clucking his tongue, he urged the appaloosa on.

It was late into the afternoon when he spotted sign of the outskirts of the rancheria. He moved slowly and deliberately, avoiding the guards that he knew were posted along the canyon walls. He could have ridden directly into the camp. But he wanted to observe before he rode in. John Daisy circled until he found the camp's herd. One of the many young boys, the *ishkiin*, that had charge of the herd, lay languishing across the back of his pony. He idly carried a switch in one hand and lazily switched away the flies. His mind was far from his responsibilities.

John Daisy waited patiently until the natural movement of the herd took the bored boy to the far side of the hundred or so animals. Hanging from the side of the appaloosa, with just a hand in the mane and a heel caught on her rump, John Daisy eased the animal into the herd. The horses moved uneasily, but quickly became accustomed to the new one. In the middle of the herd, John Daisy dropped off and melted back into the brush. Once the boy spotted the big appaloosa, he would be very puzzled that he had not noticed the animal before. When it was discovered who the animal belonged to, it would be a very good trick indeed.

Ochocama had spent two days on the high mesa, praying and meditating on the inner spirits. Now, hungry and tired, he turned his pony toward the camp. The sun was a red orb on the horizon line as he reached the pony herd. The shadows were long and dark. The young boy with the responsibility of watching the herd was standing beside a huge appaloosa mare, stroking her neck.

Ochocama slid from the back of his pony and handed him over to the bright-eyed boy. He stood for a quiet moment looking at the spotted mare. He turned and with new strength in his step he started toward the camp.

With the coming of Noch-ay-del-Klinne, the camp had doubled in size. This, just in the last two days. The old warrior strode up the grade, through the camp, many calling to him, wanting him to stop. He raised his hand in greeting but continued up the hill.

Nino was outside his wickiup, shining amusement in her eyes. She had food ready but didn't offer it as he walked up, knowing that for the moment he would forsake it. Ochocama stood before the skin flap to his door for a brief moment. He moved it aside and stepped in. In the dim interior a dark figure arose from a pile of blankets. The two men looked at each other for a moment, then moved forward into an embrace. "Chan-Deisi," the old man said, his seamed face cracking into a wide smile.

13

Miss Lucy offered the Kid a whiskey. He declined, so she only poured one. She poured about two fingers of the amber liquid in a clear glass, then filled the glass with milk from a stone decanter. It was early in the day for her. She took a sip and appraised the Kid over the rim. The Kid was smiling at her. She noted that he hadn't changed much in the year since she'd seen him. The room was elegantly fixed, all the furniture fine and expensive looking.

"It's good to see you again, Kid," she said.

"Thank you, ma'am. I always enjoy seeing a lady as pretty as yourself."

She laughed, "You're as full of it as Shonto was. Maybe even more."

"Why, thank you ma'am."

She frowned at him in a playful way. "Don't call me ma'am. It makes me feel old and I've been doin' too much of that lately."

"Yes, m… " the Kid caught himself and laughed.

She stepped across the room and the sunlight from the opened window played across her morning gown. It was a frilly gown, filled with satin and lace, buttoned from her throat to her ankles. It was markedly different than the dark-haired girl's plain frock. She looked like she was ready for the day. Her auburn hair was carefully brushed and hung to her shoulders. She wore makeup on her eyes and lips. Her cheeks had been carefully rouged. She was thinner than the Kid remembered, but still, past the carefully concealed crow's feet at her eyes and the not as firm flesh under her chin, she was still one of the best-looking women the Territory would ever see. The Kid realized that he still had his hat on. He pulled it off and ran his fingers self-consciously through his hair. He was suddenly aware of just how scruffy he must look in a parlor as elegant as this one.

"Where is your Indian friend?"

"He has gone to visit our grandfather while I came here. He ain't much of one for the city," the Kid answered.

"Your grandfather," Miss Lucy asked. "You mean the Indian you stayed with after Shonto was shot?"

"His name is Ochocama," the Kid said evenly.

Miss Lucy smiled at him. She stepped over and put her hand on his shoulder. "Now Kid, don't get riled. I don't have anything against the Apaches. You know, if it wasn't for your friend, how do you say his name?"

"John Daisy."

"Yes, John Daisy. If it wasn't for him and you, that one-eyed bastard Long Bedeaux would have killed us all." She squeezed his arm, then let her hand drop. She took another sip of her drink. "Besides, your uh, grandfather must be okay. Taking you to raise."

The Kid smiled.

Miss Lucy walked over to one of the overstuffed chairs and

sat down, crossing her legs. "But I've got to admit that you sure do remind me of Shonto. Not that you look alike, he was not as tall but beefier, and had all that dark unruly hair. But it's the way you handle yourself. Molly told me about that business downstairs. That was something Shonto would have done."

The Kid shrugged, a little uncomfortable. "Looked like Franz could use the help. I didn't know about the girl with the shotgun."

Miss Lucy nodded, "Franz usually doesn't need help." She looked at him curiously. "If your friend went to visit his grandfather, wouldn't he be all the way up to San Carlos? I thought all the Indians were on the reservation."

The Kid shrugged. "Not all of them."

Miss Lucy held his gaze a moment. "I hope your friend stays out of trouble."

The Kid smiled. "He don't know how to stay out of trouble, but I trust that if he gets in it, he'll get out of it again."

"Sit down, Kid," Miss Lucy said. "I want to talk to you about something."

The Kid looked around the room. It was a rare occasion to find himself in a room like it. The floor was covered with a deep, Oriental-styled rug that was woven with strange, intricate designs in gold and maroon. There were pretty oil paintings on the wall and vases filled with flowers. There was a brass spittoon that had never been used, and the chairs were covered with a velvet that was deep red. In the corner was a simple hard back chair that seem almost out of place. The Kid went over to it and sat down.

Miss Lucy smiled at him. "No, Kid. Not on that hard old

thing. Here, come sit on this one." She pointed to the largest of the armchairs.

The Kid obediently came over and sank into the chair. The cushion was very soft and gave way to his body until the arms on the chair curled up around him. He was more used to sitting on a horse or a forest log. He felt the chair was going to swallow him.

Miss Lucy held her glass daintily on her lap, her long nails tapping on the rim. "Did you hear that I was looking for you, or did you just happen to stop for a beer?"

"Delnorte," the Kid said. "Got news from the stage driver."

She nodded. "Kid, I want to hire you to do a job for me. I need someone I can absolutely trust."

The Kid stood up. "Miss Lucy?"

"Yes?" she said, surprised.

"Would you mind if I sat in that other chair?"

She laughed. "No. No Kid, go right ahead."

He moved over and sat on the hard back chair. "I'm flattered," he said, answering her statement.

Miss Lucy looked at this yellow haired, pale-eyed boy. Now, her eyes were serious. "I have something that I'm sending on the stage to Phoenix. I have to be absolutely certain that it gets there. I want you to go along to make sure that it does."

"Just to Phoenix?"

"There and back."

"What kind of package?"

She stood and moved to the door. She opened it and motioned to someone waiting outside. Stepping back in, she was followed by the pretty dark-haired girl from the landing. The girl's eyes were on the Kid and they were frank and probing. Her skin was a creamy pale and that made her black hair look blacker. "Kid, say hello to Molly Sand!"

The Kid came gracefully to his feet, his hat in his hand. "We've just met," he said.

The girl nodded curtly, then swept by the Kid and sat in the big, overstuffed chair the Kid had just vacated. She sat precisely the way Miss Lucy was sitting. There was a small wry smile across her face. She tilted her head at Miss Lucy, "This the boy that's gonna protect me from all the bad guys?"

"The very same," Miss Lucy said.

"Hell, miss," the girl laughed scornfully. "I barely met him, and I had to pull his acorns outa the fire already." She crossed one trim ankle over the other. "Who's gonna be protecting who?"

The Kid felt his face getting warm. His throat felt tight. He wasn't afraid to be a talker, but he wasn't much on women. Especially a woman that had the look of an angel but had the devil in her eyes. He sank back down onto the chair, trying to think of something to say.

Miss Lucy looked at the girl, faint amusement in her eyes. "I know he looks young and pretty, but when the bear climbs in the barrel, he'll do." She turned to the Kid before Molly could say anything else.

"If you turned out like Shonto, then you ain't one to sit around chewing on pleasantries, so I'll get right to the point." She leaned forward, all business now. "I'm sending Molly to Phoenix. She'll be carrying a large amount of my money. When she gets there, she'll use it to complete a deal that I've been working on for a long time."

"You trust her?" The Kid said.

"As much as I trust you." The Kid looked at the girl and she looked back.

'I've been withdrawing the money, little by little for a long time now," Miss Lucy continued. "The banker doesn't even suspect how much I've got. If he did, he'd wire his cronies in Phoenix, and they would know the hand I'm holding. I want Molly to complete the transaction so it's a done deal before it becomes public knowledge." She paused a moment then said, "If I've made any mistakes and some of these people find out that Molly has the money, they'll stop at nothing to get it."

She sat her drink aside. "Not just to get the money, but to get me."

The Kid shrugged. "Only two ways to get the money once we're on the stage. Either put someone on with us or stop it and take it." He said this to Miss Lucy, but his eyes were on Molly.

"Yes, you're right." Miss Lucy saw the Kid's look. "Don't worry 'bout her, Kid. Like I just said, I trust her as much as I do you."

The Kid smiled. "Just a little ride on the stage." He looked again at Molly Sand. "It'll be my pleasure."

"No doubt," Molly muttered.

Miss Lucy stood, smiling now. "Good, you start on the seven o'clock stage in the morning. I've told Franz to set you up with a room for the night. If you've a mind to gamble, I've told him to give you a stack of chips, just don't get drunk."

The Kid pulled his hat up on his head. "Did you ever see Shonto drunk?"

Miss Lucy looked at him.

"You didn't see him, and you won't see me." He touched the brim of his hat, "Ladies." He turned and left the room. Molly stood as if to follow.

"Wait," Miss Lucy said to the girl. "There's something else." Stepping across the room she swung a small, exquisite, painting away from the wall. Behind the wall was a recessed wall safe. She turned to look at Molly and Molly turned her back.

Spinning the tumblers, Miss Lucy opened the safe door on silent, oiled hinges. From the safe she took a small, velvet jewelry box. She brought it to the small table and set it in front of Molly.

"Go ahead," she said. Molly reached over and opened the small case. Inside the box was a locket. Small, and silver, and rather plain. A silver chain was attached, and the locket and chain were tarnished. Miss Lucy picked it up and offered it to Molly for inspection. Molly accepted it curiously.

"You can see how tarnished it has become," said Miss Lucy. The young girl was puzzled.

"I want you to wear it to Phoenix. When you get there, find a jeweler on Washington Street by the name of Johnston. He has an old Chinaman working for him. The Chinaman is the best with jewelry west of New Orleans. I want the Chinaman to restore the locket." She looked firmly at the girl. "You understand, not Johnston. Only the Chinaman."

The girl nodded, intrigued by the locket. She had known Miss Lucy for many years, since Miss Lucy had taken her in as a child. She had no idea what significance this locket held. She worked the clasp and opened the locket. On the inside was an old picture of a young, pretty woman. Molly had never seen her before. She looked up at Miss Lucy; she didn't see any family resemblance. Her eyes were full of questions, but she could tell that Miss Lucy wasn't going to explain anything.

There was a small engraving on the inside and as Molly tried to make it out, Miss Lucy said, "You take care of this. Between the money and this locket, I could replace the money. But this little bitty thing is the most valuable thing I own."

14

Nalin unfolded the soft lambskin pouch. She lifted out the tortoiseshell comb that her father had given her as a child. He had brought it to her many years ago, when he was part of the Dinee delegation that had visited the unbelievable, distant village of the Nantan-in-jah of all the whites.

Tossing her head, she let the thick dark mane cascade down her back. In the gloom of the makeshift wickiup, she sat on her knees and ran the comb through her hair. It was a ritual that gave her the sense of privacy and comfort that she needed. No one had ever been allowed to watch as she combed her hair. Not even her other women friends. Not even when her mother was alive. It was these moments that she could leave her mind open and blank. Not anxious or worried. These moments were only for herself.

Rhythmically she stroked the comb through her long hair from scalp to the small of her back, then again. Finally, after a hundred or so repetitions, she stopped and put the comb back in its special place. She took a long, deep breath, at last allowing her mind to settle again on her father.

She had food prepared for him, but she knew that once again she would almost have to force him to eat. He was so preoccupied now. The People were following in frightening numbers, and they demanded so much of him and his time. She tossed her head in anger at allowing herself to return her thoughts to this sore spot. She was deeply worried for him. Not that she didn't share his belief in the good of the dances. But he had grown gaunt and thin. He would dance all night and barely rest or take nourishment in the day.

Gar and the young men were especially trying for her. They not only danced and called upon the spirits, they wanted more. They wanted to make war. Noch-ay-del-Klinne was convinced that he could control their hot blood but Nalin was not as sure.

Rising, Nalin pulled the skin back from the door and stepped out into the quickly dying light. Looking around, she was amazed at the number of the People that had followed from San Carlos. There were people all around Noch-ay-del-Klinne's wickiup. Hundreds of people. Many had thrown up makeshift lodges, like her own, and others had simply spread their blankets on the ground.

Looking around, Nalin felt the uncomfortable feeling again. All those close by were watching her. Not staring, as it was rude for Dinee to stare, but even as these people went about their normal business, they watched every move she made. This newfound notoriety was uncomfortable.

Across from her wickiup was another one, looking much the same, hastily put up and covered with skins and whatever brush that was close. A girl of her own age sat outside, grinding the beans of mesquite into meal. As Nalin appeared, the girl sat up anxiously, as if in attendance.

Nalin looked at her, mildly. She asked, "Have you seen Noch-ay-del-Klinne, my father?"

The woman scrambled to her feet. "Yes shimaa!" she exclaimed. "He is with Gar by the waters." Before Nalin could respond the woman set off down the hill, calling over her shoulder, "I will tell him you seek him."

Nalin started to call to stop her, but irritated, let her go. She was not accustomed to being called *mother* by someone her own age. They want too much, she thought. Nalin had been well taught the ways of respect. The male elders were foremost in the families and after them, the male warriors and the female elders if their husbands were still alive. Last in the pecking order were the young wives and at the bottom were the unmarried females.

But now, she found herself treated as an elder. And not just an elder, but a diyin'. During the dances her place was next to her father's; she knew that this irritated Gar, but the People had made it so. She had become the rarest of the rare, a young, female diyin'.

She looked around the sudden camp, then turned and looked up the slope to where Ochocama's band was camped. Out of respect for his old friend, Noch-ay-del-Klinne had been very careful to leave some space between the two camps.

The last of the daylight spilled shafts of luminous gold up the slope. At the top of the slope, walking slowly toward her, was a man on horseback. It was a huge horse, white with splotches of black and a striking black mane and tail. The man rode tall in the light and even though he was a hundred yards away, Nalin felt his eyes on her. Now all other thoughts were gone from her head and her heart rose as if on a bubble to the top of her throat.

She tossed her hair back in sudden amusement, a throaty laugh coming from her chest. She turned full to meet him, her mouth opening in pleasure.

John Daisy rode the appaloosa down the slope toward the dark, backlit, silhouetted girl standing in the middle of the ramshackle camp. As he walked the appaloosa, the last rays of maroon colored light slid behind the far, cathedral shaped, mountains. In the sudden gloom, the fires of Noch-ay-del-Klinne's camp shone against the dark ground like stars on the clearest night. Using just the slightest pressure, John Daisy guided the big mare to the girl. For a moment they looked at each other, then the appaloosa stretched her neck forward with a soft nicker. Nalin held her hand out to the mare and the appaloosa nuzzled the palm of her hand. Nalin laughed and stepped closer, rubbing the side of the animal's huge neck. The appaloosa took hold of a fold of the girl's cotton blouse with its lips and tugged on her. Nalin laughed again.

"She's magnificent!" she said. "Where did you find her?"

John Daisy slid down, "In the Chiricahuas." He patted the horse. "She was undecided for three days whether she wanted to come with me or not." He grinned. "She made a good decision."

Standing next to John Daisy, Nalin noted again how tall he was. Unusually tall for Dinee. She was almost as tall. They both had been taller than the others they had grown up with. This was one of the bonds that had tied them.

"It is good to see you, little butterfly," he said.

She smiled at him. "No one has called me that in years. Now I am just Nalin, daughter to Noch-ay-del-Klinne."

"And a diyin'."

She shrugged, her smile fading. "This they tell me. I feel more a little butterfly than a diyin'." She put a hand on his arm. "You have come for the dances?"

John Daisy gave a slight shrug. "I came to visit my grandfather."

Her look was mischievous, "Only this and nothing more?"

He smiled back. "I was hoping to see you."

As she turned, she became aware that this entire end of the camp had become very aware of the two of them. Those close were trying hard to appear not to be listening. She turned back to John Daisy.

"Tie your animal to my lodge pole and we will walk. Maybe we can find a place without ears."

The summer temperature was cooling in the night air as the two of them walked out away from the camp into the darkening desert. They walked in silence for some time, making their way through the junipers until they came to an open, rising slope. Making their way up the gradual slope, John Daisy felt Nalin slip her cool hand into his. When they reached the top of the incline, there was an outcropping of rock, a ledge. They stepped out on it, facing the brilliant but receding glow in the western sky. Back below them the campfires of the village twinkled.

They stood in silence for a long time, enjoying this quiet moment together. Nalin stepped in closer, and John Daisy put his arms around her. They stood like this, holding each other from the cool night air.

Finally, Nalin spoke. It was almost a whisper. "There are times like this that I hate Ugashe'."

John Daisy looked down on her. "Why would you hate Ugashe'?"

She stepped away from him, looking into his face. "Because he is who he is, and he has taken you away from me."

John Daisy smiled at this. "If I asked you to become my wife this night, would you ride away with me to live in my lodge?"

15

Nalin looked into his dark face a long moment, then turned and looked toward the village. The night birds cried into the night. Finally, she stepped back into him, taking his arms and wrapping them around her again. "No" she said softly. "First of all, you don't have a lodge, and secondly I could not leave my father. The People need him now and he needs me."

"And thus it will always be."

These words irritated her; she pulled away from him. "You have not asked me to be your wife, nor would you. You already have a mate in Ugashe'." Her eyes flashed at him in the darkness. "You would expect me to change but you would not."

"Ugashe' is my shik'isn. That will never change."

Nalin's anger was gone as fast as it came but gone also was the feeling of the earlier moments. "Ugashe' is indaa, he is white," she said. "He cannot live in two worlds. Nor can you. You cannot choose to be Dinee and indaa. You can only be one or the other."

John Daisy looked at this beautiful girl who was at once his friend and his love, but time had changed many things.

"My choice is not only to be Ugashe''s shik'isn. It is the choice to be free or be a prisoner on the reservation."

"And I am diyin'. And being diyin' I can't hate Ugashe' because he is white, but I do hate the whites." She turned to him, a quick glint of moisture in her eye. "But mostly, I hate losing you. I hate losing my father, for I surely will. I hate losing our land and our life and the ways of the old ones. I hate the whites for taking all this from me."

John Daisy had to turn his head. He stared at the pinpricks of light below.

She spoke again, her voice like the dark velvet of the night. "I hate knowing that I probably will never carry a child in my belly. I hate knowing that I will never grow old to care for my children's children. And, most of all, I hate knowing that if I ever did take a husband, the white man would not allow him to be a man, a warrior. If he tried to be a warrior, they would kill him."

Nalin turned in the darkness and started slowly back the way they had come. John Daisy followed silently. The moon was now cresting the far eastern mountains and the drums of the dance had begun far below.

They walked in silence. After several long moments Nalin asked, "I did not see Ugashe'. Is he here?"

John Daisy said, "No. He has gone to the white man's town to help a friend."

"That is good," she said.

"Why is that good?" he asked.

"Ugashe' is white."

"Ugashe' is Ochocama's grandson."

Nalin shook her head. "Gar does not care about that. He

would only see Ugashe''s white skin."

"Gar," John Daisy snorted. "Gar would not be alive if it were not for Ugashe'."

"Yes, and Gar has never forgiven him for it." She continued, "Do not take Gar lightly. He is my father's right arm and has become very powerful. The young ones follow him more than my father. Gar believes that my father's vision was proof that the spirits will return to help him drive the indaa from our land."

At this, John Daisy growled low in his chest. This startled Nalin and she laughed in surprise.

John Daisy spoke softly. "Gar would do well to beware. Ugashe' is grown now. He was taught by the old wolf Shonto Page and by our grandfather, Ochocama." He turned to look at her; his voice was hard. "Ugashe' is the most dangerous man I know. More dangerous than Ochocama, more dangerous than Tatsahdasaygo, the Quick Killer. Gar would be wise to avoid him as the rabbit avoids the coyote."

They were on the outskirts of the camp now and the wickiups were empty. All of the people had converged on the center of the camp. A huge fire was burning, and the drums and the singing had filled the night.

Nalin took John Daisy's wrist and led him around the edge of the camp until they reached her lodge. The appaloosa whinnied at the scent of John Daisy. Nalin bade John Daisy to wait, then she quickly disappeared into the wickiup. A few short moments went by and when she reappeared, she was dressed in a pale, ghostly shaded, fringed dress with intricate designs embroidered across the shoulders and down the front. Her face was painted with pale ash colors.

"Come," she said. "You will see the power of the dances. My father will be very pleased that you have come."

Leaving the appaloosa tied, John Daisy silently followed Nalin into the village. At the center of the camp, there were a hundred men and women gathered in a great circle around an open area. In the center of the open space was the huge fire. Noch-ay-del-Klinne was beside the fire, head back, eyes closed, dancing the ancient steps and chanting the old words.

Beside him was Gar, his face glistening with sweat, the jagged scar pale against his cheek. As those on the edge of the crowd recognized Nalin, a cry went up and hands took hold of her, thrusting her forward as the crowd parted. She cast a look back toward John Daisy but already they were separated, and the people moved her to the center.

John Daisy watched as she began the movements, her eyes closing, her voice lost in the noise, her mouth moving to the words. He felt the power of the longing that was in these people. Looking from face to face he could feel their need washing over him. The rhythm of the drums pounded into his soul, and he could physically feel the desire to call to the spirits for help. But he did not move and after a long time he turned and quietly slipped away and back up the slope.

He untied the appaloosa and rode her to the herd that was corralled in Ochocama's mesquite corral. He turned her loose and walked slowly back to Ochocama's lodge, his heart filled with many emotions. He knew that his grandfather had decided not to attend the dances, so he was not surprised to see light coming from around the crack of the doorway not covered by the skin. His grandfather was still up.

He cleared his throat to announce his arrival, then slipping back the skin he stepped into the lodge. There was a small fire glowing in the center. His grandfather, looking old and withered in the firelight, sat across from the door. He was smoking his pipe. To his right side, sitting cross-legged, sat a man with a thick moustache and a larger than normal nose. His campaign hat lay on the ground beside him. The firelight glinted off his polished boots and the handle of his service revolver.

"Aw, John Daisy," the man said, climbing to his feet, his hand extended.

"Lieutenant Gatewood," a surprised John Daisy returned, in his slurring English, taking the man's outstretched hand in the awkward custom of the whites.

16

Gar was pleased with the fervor of the people. He gradually made his way through the dancers until he was beside Disalin, a true disciple and one not afraid to shed blood. Once he had Disalin's attention he leaned into the man and said, just loud enough for him but no one else, "It is tonight. Take your men and be at the road before daylight. Strike hard."

There were ten that followed Disalin from the camp at the hint of first light. Disalin led the group, but it was Gar's vision of what should be that spurred every man on. Disalin eagerly rode his pony across the valley, his veins pounding with the knowledge that the long-awaited day had come.

Disalin was a true believer and had followed Noch-ay-del-Klinne from the beginning. But Disalin had come to believe, as Gar, that Noch-ay-del-Klinne did not have the strength to see his vision to the end. Nalin was but a woman and therefore not capable of battle. No, only Gar and Disalin would have the spirit to lead the warriors against the whites.

Disalin rode proudly at the head of the young men. He saw himself as the heir to great warriors that had come before.

Ochocama had been one, but now was old and feeble. Mangus Coloradas and Cochise were long dead. Loco and Chato hid in the Sierra Madres of the Nachaiye' and Geronimo was still running. It was Disalin that rode this day, wearing the magic of his spirit shirt. It was Disalin that would strike the first blow.

After a long ride over the high mountains, the band of ten came to the place that Gar had described. The young men wiped their ponies down and rested them. They stripped to nothing but loincloths and painted their bodies with their personal magic. They painted their magic symbols on the shoulders and rumps of their ponies.

Later, after the sun was high, the young one that was watching at the crest came racing down the hill. The prey was but two miles away and approaching quickly. Disalin turned to his warriors. He raised his stolen carbine above his head and screamed his warrior's cry. All of them began to yell and whoop, racing their ponies in circles. Disalin pulled his pony out of the bunch and led the band down to their chosen place of ambush.

Earlier that day the Kid had his belly full of a two-bit breakfast and was sitting in the shade outside the stationhouse of the Gilmer and Salisbury stage line. He was picking his teeth with a broom bristle when he saw Molly Sand and Franz coming up the street.

On the other side, the driver was talking nervously about the difficulty of the Yarnell hill. Talking about how he was happy he didn't have that run today. Talking like you do when you feel you're expected to talk but you don't know the person you're talking to. His talk was directed at a small group of men that had gathered, waiting to take the stage. The driver this time wasn't

Sam Perkins. Today the driver was a big-bellied man with a strong, drooping moustache that covered his mouth. He had the horses in the trace and was securing the luggage of the passengers at the top. There would be a guard this run. A small, stringy looking, sour man. He stood to the side holding a Spencer in the crook of his arm. He had a wad of tobacco in his jaw, as he insolently watched the driver do all the preparation. He was a shooter, not a skinner.

The Kid watched, amused at the change that came over the men as Molly Sand walked up. With Franz right beside her, you'd have to be blind stupid not to know who she was. And this morning she was a vision, dressed in a full traveling dress with a small hat pinned on top of her dark ringlets of hair.

The passengers all tipped their hats and smiled broadly. Molly made her way over to the Kid and stood in front of him. The Kid got to his feet, touching the brim of his hat. He stood with one fluid motion without any excess of movement. The Kid nodded good mornin' and she nodded in return. She turned and dismissed Franz. He gave the Kid a knowing look, then turned and walked back down the street. Molly moved to the side with the shade and waited silently. Her hand kept coming back to fondle a tarnished silver locket that hung by a silver chain around her throat.

The Kid sat again, stretching his legs out, waiting. In a short while the driver set the call and they all crammed into the confines of the Concord. It appeared to be large from the outside but putting five men and a full skirted lady on the inside was a close affair. The Kid found himself pressed against the wall next to the door. Molly was pressed against him, and a mustached man in a derby on the other side. Across from them was a tall slender man in a broadcloth suit, and two men that had the roughhewn look of ranchers. Beneath the pulled-down brim of his hat, the Kid studied them all, studying their eyes and boots and the calluses on their hands. He could smell the ether that had recently cleaned the slender man's broadcloth suit. The two ranchers knew each other and talked of cattle and the drought.

Once the vehicle began to move, the slender man pulled his hat down and appeared to sleep. The man in the derby gazed out the other window. Molly sat with her eyes on her hands, her hands in her lap. The Kid sat as comfortably as he could, with the beaded sheath holding his Winchester sitting butt down between his moccasined feet. The Walker Colt was on his belt, but he had to slide it more around to his side for comfort. Shonto's Colt was pressed against Molly, but she didn't complain.

As the day wore on, the slender man accomplished the sleep he was feigning, his mouth hanging open. The ranchers continued to talk and the derbied man joined in once in a while. He told them he was a reporter. Molly finally closed her eyes, her head gently bobbing to the movement of the stage. The Kid stared out the window, waiting. Not much else to do.

Half a day had passed when suddenly, the Kid was jerked awake by the report of a rifle discharging, then the sight of the body of the stringy guard dropping past the window and bouncing across the ground. Simultaneously, there was an explosion of shots and the screams of Apaches. The stage swerved and the Kid had the Walker in his hand. The other men were scrambling to pull their pistols from their clothing. The man with the derby was digging frantically in his satchel. The stage was rocking violently, and the Kid could feel bullets hitting the stage. The horses were running flat out now, and the driver's voice was screaming at them above the rackety noise of the stage.

The Kid had no target from his window. He was amazed they were being attacked. There hadn't been an attack like this in the last few years. Out the other window he saw a painted pony come racing up. The derbied man had dug out a little five-shot pocket pistol and started popping away at the rider. The Apache was racing alongside the stage, brandishing a rifle, holding it one-handed. The Indian dropped back as the man began shooting. Then as the man had fired all five shots and was fumbling in his pocket for more shells, the Apache charged up to the window. His painted face was screaming and ugly. He held his rifle straight out. The Kid moved, pushing Molly down and trying to pull the derbied man out of the line of the rifle. The rifle exploded and the man's head snapped back, sending the derby and blood and flesh spraying across Molly's dress. She screamed as the man slumped into her.

The Indian reigned back and the Kid put a shot into the horse. It stumbled, then pulled out of sight. Both ranchers and the tall slender man were firing out the windows. The Kid was sitting on the wrong side to get any kind of shot. His right hand had to reach across Molly, who was doubled over making herself as small as possible. He switched the pistol to his left hand and fired out the window above Molly. Now the painted Apaches were riding ahead, alongside the team. They were intent on bringing down the driver. The horses were running wildly, flat out. The coach was bucking and careening on the rough dirt road. The Kid felt a shift and he knew they were off the trail.

He could tell the driver was down. The coach began to sway violently back and forth, and on each swing it seemed that the next one would send the coach over. The men had quit firing and were desperately holding on. Molly had a death grip on the Kid's arm and the Kid shifted the pistol back to his other hand and had his left hand on the door lever. The rear end of the stage was sliding when it hit a rock, the wheels flew up into the air and came down with a sickening crash. The coach violently rocked to two wheels, first on the Kid's side, then it rocked the other way and this time kept going.

When the momentum went the other way, the Kid hit the door handle with his left hand and grabbed a fist full of Molly's dress with the other. As the coach tipped its final time the Kid flew out the door dragging Molly behind him. The coach crashed to its side with the men trapped and screaming inside. The terrified horses dragged the wagon for a hundred feet before they were jerked to a sudden halt.

17

The Kid and Molly were slammed to the ground and lost their grip on each other. The Kid bounced and rolled and came up with a mouth full of dirt but kept a grip on his pistol. The Winchester was under him. The breath was near out of him, but he didn't stop. He rolled to his feet spitting. He saw that they'd had a whole lot of luck. Before it had gone down, the coach had been running beside a dry wash on their side of the wagon. Because of the broken ground that had finally upset it, the attackers had been riding, almost to a man, on the other side of the coach. Now they were milling around the wreck, whooping and screaming a hundred feet away. The Kid took three steps and handed the dazed girl his Winchester. With the Walker in his left and Shonto's Colt in his right he turned and began firing both pistols so rapidly that the sound was continuous. Two Indians went down, and another bullet struck a pony in the shoulder. The horse screamed and began to buck, scattering the other riders.

Molly was to her knees and was looking around at the ground, stunned. In one motion the Kid holstered Shonto's Colt and taking Molly around the waist, swept her up off the ground, her gripping the Winchester. Directly behind was the wash, each side thickly covered with brush. Holding the girl in the air, the Kid took three steps backward and crashed into the mass of the thicket. He pushed his way backward, forcing them through the branches. The sharp thorns and branches tore at their skin and clothes.

Suddenly, they popped through and the Kid, losing his balance, fell into the wash, landing in the soft sand, the girl on top. Struggling to his feet he pulled the girl up and forced her forward up the wash. "Hurry, run," he urged. The Apaches were screaming in rage and there was no more firing from the other passengers. A few of the Apaches were now moving to the other side of the brush. They were firing wildly into the wash, but the Kid and Molly were already moving, and the Apaches couldn't see them. They ran hard for a few long yards, then the Kid pulled Molly up the other side of the bank. Again, turning his back to shield the girl, he forced his way through the deep brush. Once up on the other side, he led the girl away from the wash, then turning abruptly he began dragging her back the way they had come. He looked at her, putting his finger to his lips. He knew this wouldn't trick the attackers for long, but it might buy some time. The ground opened out a bit then climbed to a small ridge. The Kid got them around the ridge as fast as possible, using the outcropping to shield them. Over his shoulder he could see black smoke boiling up from where the stage was. He could hear the whoops of triumph but there were no more shots.

He took the Winchester from the girl and stuffing the sheath in his belt and the rifle under his arm, he reloaded the pistols while they moved. He shoved the pistols back into their holsters and began loading the Winchester. The girl's traveling shoes weren't meant for this kind of traveling. But Molly was game and stayed up with him.

The Kid admired her toughness. She had a skinned spot on her forehead, and on occasion she held her elbow. Every once in a while, he would glance at her. He knew that if she faded now, they would be in deep trouble. Her dress was ripped and filthy, but she doggedly kept up without complaining or wilting.

For over a mile, they moved as quickly as they could in the rough terrain. The Kid finally stopped to give the girl a rest and to study their back trail. Their path had been moving on a gradual incline and now he stood stock still, studying the land behind for movement.

The girl was looking at him, her hand to her throat, "I've lost the locket," she said wretchedly.

He looked at her in amazement. "A locket," he muttered. He reached to the top of his knee-high moccasin and pulled his skinning knife. It was razor sharp with a seven-inch blade. The girl turned and studied the back trail alongside of him. "Have we lost them?"

"Not hardly," the Kid answered. He tossed the knife so that it stuck, quivering, into a barrel cactus beside the girl. "You're leaving pieces of torn dress on both sides of the trail."

Molly Sand looked at the knife, puzzled.

"You need to lose them petticoats and trim your dress up to knee high for travel. We have a long way to walk."

Molly looked at the Kid with cool eyes, then without hesitation, she hiked her dress up and started shucking the petticoats. Startled, the Kid felt his face flush and he turned away.

The girl said "What's the matter, Kid? You ain't never seen a girl's undies before?"

"Ain't a habit I've had a chance to enjoy much, ma'am," The Kid said, self-conscious about his blushing face.

He glanced at her as she began sawing away at her dress. She had the Kid's mind wandering so that he almost missed seeing a cactus wren suddenly veer away from a nearby saguaro. The Apache came up off the ground screaming, charging forward. He had an old single shot carbine to his shoulder. It exploded and something ticked the Kid's hat. He levered the Winchester and fired at almost the same moment hitting the man in the chest and knocking him sideways into the dust.

Molly screamed and as the Kid turned, another one hit him from behind. Because he was turning, the second Apache hit him a glancing blow instead of flush. It did knock the Kid sideways and to one knee. The man's momentum took him over the top of the Kid and as he went over his fingers grabbed the Kid's long hair. It jerked the Kid around and slammed him to the ground. The Winchester went skidding in the dirt. The Kid and the short burly Indian scrambled to their feet. The Apache came up with a long-wicked blade in his hand. The Kid's hip pistol was held by a leather thong over the hammer. He reached to the belly Colt and the holster was empty. The Apache lunged, the knife outstretched, his eyes full of hate. The Kid dodged and kicked him in the stomach. His breath exploding, he turned, bending forward. The Kid hammered him right behind the ear with both fists. The Apache stumbled forward from the force of the blow, both hands extended. As he started to fall, he was headed downhill. He began that funny little run a man does when he's lost his balance. He was headed directly at Molly.

She screamed, pushing her hands forward to ward off the man. The Kid's knife was still in one of them. The man ran right into it, the force of his momentum driving it deep into his shoulder. He screamed as he hit the ground. The Kid stepped forward and kicked him in the head. He flopped over with a groan. The Kid yanked the knife from the man's shoulder and deftly slit his throat.

Molly stood to one side, a hand to her mouth, her eyes wide. "Oh my God," she groaned.

The Kid scooped up the Walker and the Winchester, crouched low, ready for another attack. His eyes scoured the brush, but no other came. There was no sound. The Kid stepped to the second man's body and flipped him over. He bent down and studied him. He went to the first man and studied him also. Molly was staring at him, her face white and sick looking.

"What are you doing," she said.

"Seeing if I know them," the Kid said softly.

Molly turned suddenly and leaned down. She began to retch then vomited into the grama grass.

"Guess we both seen something new today," the Kid said.

18

Lieutenant Gatewood sat cross-legged beside the small fire in Ochocama's lodge, suppressing the urge to smooth back his moustache. He knew he must remain calm and in control of this. Show no nervousness, he told himself.

He concentrated on keeping his face impassive. He concentrated on the old warrior across the small fire. They had been sitting in silence for some time now. Gatewood had come into the rancheria alone. Walking through the deserted camp he saw one wickiup showing light. He recognized the marking of the tanned hide that was the door. He had been given good directions by the Dinee scout that had infiltrated the camp, then had come back to report. The old man had shown no surprise when Gatewood had stepped through the door. They had looked at each other, then the old man waved for Gatewood to have a seat. The old man picked up his pipe and lit it. He puffed on it, then offered it to the Lieutenant. Gatewood accepted it. He puffed on it twice, then offered it back.

"I have come to talk," he said.

Ochocama said, "Be patient. We will wait for him."

Gatewood wondered who they waited for? Noch-ay-del-Klinne? Gar? Whoever it was, he had to still himself and wait.

Finally, he heard movement outside the lodge. It was one man, leading a horse. It was a horse with a deep foot. A large horse. After a moment there was a coughing noise as the man outside cleared his throat to announce himself. The skin flap was thrust backward and a tall, young Apache stepped in. The old man's face lit up and Gatewood knew they had been waiting for this young man. He was surprised that he knew who this man was. This was Ochocama's grandson, the son of Alchesay. The one that rode with Shonto Page's boy.

"John Daisy," he said, rising, holding his hand out. The young man took it in the awkward, soft way of the Apache. As if not sure what to do with the hand once it was in the grasp.

"Lieutenant Gatewood," John Daisy returned in his slurring English.

Gatewood smiled, liking this. "It is good to meet a friend," he said in his broken Dinee.

John Daisy smiled, pleased. He didn't know many white men who spoke his language. Delnorte and Ugashe', a few others.

Ochocama waved his arm. "Sit," the old man said. The two men obeyed, taking seats across the small, smokeless mesquite fire. Now Ochocama repacked his pipe. Taking his time, packing it with the treasured tobacco that Gatewood's scout had brought him as a gesture of good will. The two young men waited as the old man got the pipe fired, waited as he took his deep draws, knowing that this had to come first.

During this time, Gatewood studied the young Indian. Major Tom Redding, whose wife Abigail had been saved by John Daisy and the Kid at Delnorte's Station, had described him well. He had said the boy looked like he had been made out of hard, flat slabs of copper. Gatewood could see the high cheek bones and other signs of Comanche blood from his mother's side. Gatewood's eyes strayed to the scar tissue on the upper right of the neck muscle. This, where John Daisy had been shot off his horse at Delnorte's when Redding's wife had been taken. When Long Bedeaux and his killers had taken the stage looking for the thieving Indian Agent, Emmett Teas. Major Redding had described John Daisy well, and the young, yellow haired, white boy that had been raised by Shonto Page. Shonto Page and the old warrior across from him. Hell of a childhood, Gatewood thought.

Gatewood had been surprised that John Daisy had known who he was. Sitting, waiting, he surmised that John Daisy must have at least some contacts with his scouts. Or some information that had come from them. Most knew that Gatewood had been the Chief of Scouts for the last two years, out of Fort Grant and now Fort Apache. Gatewood glanced at the old chief. He was thinking how other contemporaries were naive to think the Apache are unaware. All fifteen thousand of them probably know every officer we have and who and where they are. Finally, Ochocama spoke, and it was a staccato burst directed to the young Apache. It went too fast for Gatewood to comprehend; the lieutenant only picked up the words *you talk* and *hair-face*.

John Daisy turned to the white soldier; he spoke in his slurring English, "My grandfather says that he has welcomed you to his home. He says that he knows you and knows you to be a man of honor. He wishes to know why you have chosen to come?" John Daisy leaned forward, saying, "I speak to you now.

My grandfather knows little of your language, but he is no fool. At his cry, you would be dead. There are many that would welcome the chance." Gatewood looked impassively into the dark, bottomless eyes of the young man. John Daisy continued, "He is of the old ways, but he is smart enough to know that you and Nantan Lupan have purposely let him be. This is all he wants, just to be let alone. To live his life, to have his people live their lives in peace. Why do you come to him now?"

Gatewood spread his hands out in a sign of supplication. "It is not Ochocama that I am sent for. It is for the Dancer of Shadows. I am sent to bring Noch-ay-del-Klinne back to the agency."

"Noch-ay-del-Klinne is surrounded by his people. If you tried to take him there will be trouble."

The soldier nodded. "I know that. Unfortunately, Nantan Lupan is no longer our chief. There is a new chief. His name is Carr. I am under strict orders to bring the diyin' back to San Carlos. He will have to return. It is too bad that he has exposed your grandfather to this. I'm afraid that he will have to go to San Carlos also."

John Daisy looked at the man a long time. A deep sadness filled his heart. He finally turned and spoke to Ochocama. He explained what Gatewood had said. When he finished, Ochocama remained silent, drawing on his pipe, his thoughts seemingly far away. John Daisy turned back to the soldier. "Noch-ay-del-Klinne, himself, will cause you no trouble. He is' diyin', a Dreamer, not a warrior. He is a reasonable man, but he believes that the People need the dances. Your trouble will come from others. From his followers."

"Like Gar."

John Daisy nodded. "Yes, Gar."

Again the soldier held out his hands, palms up. "It is not up to me. I follow the orders of our nantan. General Carr has assigned this problem to Colonel Tibbet. He will insist that all Dinee' stay on the reservation. And also that all that are off, return. He would send the Army here to enforce that. He is a very ambitious man. I am but a soldier, I must obey. I came alone tonight to show your grandfather my personal good faith. This Colonel Tibbet would just as soon that I came here with a troop and drive everyone back. I know that Noch-ay-del-Klinne would listen to one voice, and that is of your grandfather. I came to convince your grandfather to use his voice of reason to persuade Noch-ay-del-Klinne to return. If Noch-ay-del-Klinne returns, his people will follow."

Ochocama inclined his head toward John Daisy, seeking a translation. John Daisy repeated what Gatewood had said. Ochocama took the statements impassively. He sat silently for a time, then spoke. While speaking, he looked at John Daisy. When he finished he lay the pipe aside and Gatewood knew that the interview was over.

John Daisy said, "My grandfather is flattered at your exaggerated views of his powers of persuasion. He says that Noch-ay-del-Klinne does hear voices, but they are not his. He says that because you have come to his lodge in good faith, he will take you to speak to Noch-ay-del-Klinne in the morning sun. He cannot guarantee that Noch-ay-del-Klinne will listen."

Ochcocama stood and so did the two younger men. Gatewood put his hand out to each of the men and they in turn took it. He placed his campaign hat on and touched its curled brim in a form of salute. He swung back the skin that covered the entrance and stepped out into the night.

19

Disalin sat astride his pony and watched with satisfaction as his warriors pulled the corpses from the ruined Concord coach. He sat to the side, allowing them their pleasure as they mutilated the bodies, gouging the white eyes out and shoving severed testicles into dead, gaping mouths. He looked to the wash, waiting for the shots that would signify that the man and woman that had miraculously escaped had been caught by the two he had sent. He was irritated at how long it was taking. Then he heard the report of a Springfield carbine, followed closely by that of another rifle. Then there were no other shots.

He nudged his pony over to the stage and watched as his men went through the belongings of the dead passengers. After time had passed, he grew even more irritated. Maybe there was sport with the girl. When he could wait no longer, he ordered his men into the brush to find them. As he wheeled his pony, something shiny in the long grama grass caught his eye. He swung down and reached into the long grass, finding a tarnished silver locket with a broken clasp. He turned it round and round, studying it. He smiled. The magic that was once the white squaw's was now his.

It took no time to find the trail of the white woman. Cotton threads littered the thicket of palo verdes and salt bushes. It was rough and rocky ground and the warriors had to picket their ponies and continue on foot. He left the youngest with the ponies and the other young ones were eager and rushed out in front. In a few minutes, they came to a sudden halt, a cry of despair coming from their lips. There in the brush were the lifeless bodies of their two companions.

Disalin studied the ground around the bodies with a sense of uneasiness, his mouth tight with caution. He had just had a glimpse of the man and woman as they disappeared into the brush. There was something about the man that was gnawing at him. Something old and familiar. Studying the bodies of his two men, he saw the long, broken, strands of blond hair, still clutched in the dead hand of Toos-day-zay. The sight of the long yellow hair jumped out as a warning, but it was something that he couldn't yet put his finger on. He saw the pile of petticoats and the torn dress and realized this might not be as easy as he had assumed. All around him, his band was filled with revenge and anger, crying out for blood.

He put his best tracker out in front, and the tracker soon found the sign leading away, toward the rockiest, roughest area. Within a few yards, where the sign became scarce, the sign of two became the sign of one. In another twenty yards all sign disappeared onto rocky ground.

The Apaches spread out, moving cautiously, their eyes narrowed, their hands on their knives and their carbines. They moved silently through the jumbled boulders and scrub brush. Their eyes constantly scanning the ground, searching for any displaced rock or scrape of moccasin, or wisp of thread.

After a while it became unbelievable. A few minutes more passed, and it became supernatural. The white man and woman had disappeared into nothing. Very few white men and no white women could disappear like this. One of the younger Indians turned to another close by and under his breath muttered "chiidn!" The other young one's eyes widened with fear. Disalin was in a silent rage now, his murderous eyes sweeping every crack and cranny and bush. He swore to himself these two would die slowly when they were found.

The Kid was working his way from boulder to boulder, moving as quickly as he could with the girl on his back. He knew that if he had bad luck, it would be very bad, with him weighed down and his hands occupied. But this was a trick that he and John Daisy had used since childhood. Making two sets of footprints into only one. It didn't work on soft ground where the depth of the footprint would give it away, but on this hard packed desert floor, and working his way from boulder to boulder, their sign had virtually disappeared.

The Kid chose his path carefully, choosing the most awkward and difficult trail. This slowed him considerably, but again, he was counting on a little luck to remain undiscovered. He knew those that followed would expect them to be in a headlong flight. Shonto had taught him to pick the most treacherous and difficult way. Shonto had taught that it was human nature to choose the easiest path. Just like water running downhill. Therefore, any tracker would assume the same and lose a lot of time before the true, harder path was discovered.

The Kid came suddenly to a steep slide, where a million years before, half of this small mountain had lost its grip and slid into the gully below. The Kid stood a moment studying it, the girl almost choking him with her grip around his neck. He started up the rock fall.

"What the hell are you doin," Molly breathed.

"Climbing," the Kid forced out, his breath coming in short bursts.

"Brilliant!" Molly snorted. "He's a genius," she said to the rocks around her. "But why?"

The Kid took a few more steps before he could answer. "'Cause they wouldn't do it, so they won't expect me to do it."

Moving higher up, Molly tightened her grip and began to hum a little tuneless song. It was really steep now and the Kid finally had to stop and physically pull her arm away from his throat to breathe. "You're chokin' me."

Her mouth was next to his ear. She was looking down. "If I fall, you're goin' with me, you bastard."

The Kid turned his head a little; he had to laugh. "Two things," he said. "One, you don't know my parents! Two, if we fall, I'll be on top." He turned and started up again. She was silent, but she lightened her grip.

Halfway up the slide, the Kid crawled over a large smooth chunk of granite and saw what might save them. Between the boulder and the side of the mountain was a space. It was seven feet long and about two and a half feet wide, tapering at each end. He didn't see it until he was right on it. With luck the Apaches wouldn't get that close. They would have to be in it before they saw it. A few feet on either side and it would be invisible. And if they were discovered it was a good place to defend. At some time in the distant past, this chunk of rock had shifted and the fissure between it and the mountain that had formed had filled with dirt and dust and soft blown leaves and a scattering of pine needles.

The Kid gingerly set Molly down, cautioning her to place her feet on the hard rock instead of the soft loam. He turned to look. The opening could not be seen from the bottom or either side of the rock. You had to be standing directly on the boulder. He looked up, then smiled. The slope of the slide was at a severe angle, and from above, he calculated you could see the top of the rock but would be completely unaware of the fissure between it and the mountain side.

Molly was sweeping the loose tendrils of hair from her face and started to step up to look around. Down the canyon, through the junipers, the Kid saw a small slice of movement. Reaching up, he grabbed a handful of the back of what was left of her dress and pulled her down on top of him. His left hand smothered the startled cry that had begun its escape. He held her firm against him, lying full length in the long, narrow crack.

In a short moment, she stopped struggling and when he was certain she would make no noise, he released her, whispering, "Silence."

They lay silently, hearing only their own breathing, smelling the dark loam that likely had not been touched by another human being for centuries, if ever. After what seemed an eternity, the Kid heard the whisper of moccasin leather on the rocks close by. Molly heard it too. She stiffened, then began to tremble. She turned silently to the Kid her eyes wide with fear. The fear had brought tears to her eyes, and she lay struggling for control, staring into his eyes from three inches away. Now they could hear the Apaches moving below them. The Kid tightened his arms around the girl, trying to give her silent comfort. He could sense panic rising in the girl like red in a thermometer. He was suddenly afraid that she would cry out.

He did what he had to do. He kissed her.

Molly's eyes widened even more, her mouth firm against his. She didn't resist and as they stared across less than an inch at each other, the Kid could feel her body relax. Slowly, after a very long moment, he withdrew his lips from hers. The searching killers were momentarily forgotten as he studied the beautiful girl. Her lips were slightly parted and black ringlets of hair clustered around her flushed face.

The Kid could hear the briefest of faint sounds as the Apaches moved further away. After a time, Molly began to squirm, trying to get more comfortable. They lay stretched on the soft cushion of rotting leaves and pine needles. They were touching from breastbone to knee, their faces just inches apart. Molly leaned forward and put her lips against the Kid's ear.

"How long must we stay here?" she whispered.

Now they shifted their heads and the Kid put his lips into the soft black hair covering her ear. "Till dark."

Now her turn, "That's at least two hours, what do we do till then?"

The Kid shrugged, "Nothing to do but wait."

She brought her head around until their noses were almost touching. Suddenly there came a small wry smile and the tip of her pink tongue brushed across her lips. She kissed him, kissing him hard. This time her eyes were closed, and her mouth was open. When she pulled away, she said, "I can think of something."

20

Major Tiffany sat cooling his heels in the great General Carr's anteroom. The major was fifty-five years of age. His hair was graying rapidly and curling in the back. His face was leather and lines. His hat was in his lap and the tan line stopped just above his eyebrows. This left the thinning part at the top looking milky white. He had served in the Arizona / New Mexico Territory for fifteen years. He had served under many commanders during his long career. In 1863, at Fredericksburg, he had participated in the battle of Marie's Heights and being the only officer not slaughtered, was close enough to Burnside that he knew the regiment, and had been battlefield promoted to captain.

Later, when Lee invaded Pennsylvania, he had been awarded the quicksilver rank of colonel for holding the stone wall that protected Chamberlain's flank in the battle for Little Round Top. But that war was long over and now in this parched and dusty hellhole, he held the rank of major and the title of Indian Agent, San Carlos Reservation.

As he waited, he was thinking he had not given Crook enough credit. He hadn't liked Crook's ways. His familiarity with the Apache, his loose discipline, but now, the major had to admit that Crook was preferable to the fat popinjay that now commanded the territory. Tiffany was aware that the report he brought was not going to win him any popularity contests with this general. He looked at the closed door to the general's office, thinking that even if he walked through it a major, he wasn't sure that he'd walk back out with the same rank. Tiffany had long ago given up his ambition to make brevet. He had learned in the last several months that General Carr promoted only General Carr.

Finally, the general's adjutant came and escorted him into the great one's office. Carr stood behind his outsized desk, gazing out the window that overlooked the compound. He didn't turn or acknowledge the major's entrance. To the side, along the wall, by the bookcase, stood Colonel Tibbet.

The little colonel. Known behind his back as the hatchet. Major Tiffany hadn't known that the colonel would be there but knew that he shouldn't be surprised. The joke in the barracks was that if Carr came to a sudden and unexpected halt at the same time that the little colonel sneezed, the general would get an enema.

Major Tiffany stepped to the regulation spot at the front of the desk and stood stiffly at attention. His eyes were straight ahead and for a long moment no one spoke. Tiffany waited patiently. He had done this a thousand times before on a hundred different parade grounds.

Finally, the rotund general turned and looked at the Indian agent. The general was of average height but possessed a great girth. In his wide and fleshy face, his eyes were narrow and set close together. His complexion was ruddy. His hair was wispy and white, with old-fashioned muttonchop sideburns on his pink cheeks. If his eyes could have been kindlier, he could have been the image of St. Nicholas.

"As you were," he said gruffly.

Major Tiffany went to parade rest.

The general was irritated. "For God's sake man, just relax. What's on your mind."

Tiffany relaxed a moment, his mind going over the opening that he had practiced. "We have a problem, sir," he said evenly. "A problem that I know you are aware of, as we have talked of it before. However, in my judgement the problem is getting out of hand." Carr was looking at him stonily. Tiffany hurried on, "I'm afraid, sir, that the problem has gone beyond the resources of the troop assigned to the agency."

The general glanced at the little colonel. Colonel Tibbet stepped away from the wall. "What's the problem," he asked softly.

The major glanced at the colonel, then back to the general. Tibbet said, "Well, go ahead, man. What's the problem?"

"It's the Apaches, sir. It's these religious dances, what they call the shadow dances, sir. I know that at first you said to leave them be because they were religious meetings, and we didn't want to give the wrong impression to the civilians."

"Yes, yes, I remember. So, what are they doing now?"

"Well, sir, quite frankly sir, the whole thing has gotten out of hand."

"You already said that major," Colonel Tibbet said, his voice cool.

"Yes, sir." Tiffany paused a moment. "At first there were just a few. Their medicine man, Noch-ay-del-Klinne, and his daughter, and a few others. Then more and more began to attend. But there still wasn't any real problem. Then, about a month or so ago, this Noch-ay-del-Klinne and two of his followers slipped off the reservation and supposedly went into their holy mountains, which I think is up in the Catalinas. Anyway, they said they saw some kind of vision."

"Vision?" Carr cocked an eyebrow. He moved away from the bright window and around his desk.

Major Tiffany shrugged. "What they say, sir. But now, not one of them will talk about it. Not even the scouts, not even Dandy Jim. When we ask, they just look at us and won't respond. And that's part of the problem, sir. The scouts, I mean."

"Lieutenant Gatewood's scouts?" Carr said.

Tiffany nodded, "Yeah, Gatewood's scouts. I mean some of those boys have been with us for ten years or better. Crook used them in every campaign."

"General Crook," General Carr corrected.

"Yessir, General Crook. What I'm trying to say, general, is those boys have proven their loyalty. We've even used them to track down their own kin. Their loyalty has never been a question."

"But now?" Colonel Tibbet prompted.

Major Tiffany nodded. "But now, they won't even talk to us about this. Something is going on. I sense an insurrection and we have to stop it."

General Carr sat at his desk and opened a silver box. He took out a tailor-made cigarette. The regulars called it a pimp stick.

He said, "Major, I'm not quite sure you have brought me to understand what you are talking about." He lit the cigarette. "Insurrection is a very strong word."

Tiffany began to speak, then caught himself and took a breath, getting control. "Sir, this religious thing has stirred up the Apaches like nothing I've seen in ten years. And now, this Noch-ay-del-Klinne has taken to slipping off the reservation and holding these dances in areas the tribes consider sacred. Unfortunately, there are more and more of the tribe going with him each time he does it. And this includes the scouts."

"The scouts go too?" Colonel Tibbet said. "That is against standing orders."

Tiffany nodded.

"This is insurrection," Carr declared, puffing on the cigarette.

"We haven't had any trouble yet, but it's a matter of time."

"Yet!" The general repeated.

Colonel Tibbet came over and hitched a leg on the corner of the general's desk, something that Major Tiffany would never have dreamed of doing. The colonel's eyes were on Major Tiffany, but his mind was racing. He turned this over, looking at it. He had spent the last three years lamenting the fact that he had been assigned to the only remaining area where a soldier could see some action but came too late to see any. He knew the fastest way to promotion was in action. Crook had already taken all the glory.

"Insurrection," he repeated under his breath.

Tiffany turned to him, "Sir?"

Colonel Tibbitt straightened, almost smiling. He saw it now. He glanced at General Carr, hoping the old, fat fool didn't see this the way he was seeing it.

"I can't see how one old medicine man could be much trouble to our troops," he said coolly to the major.

Major Tiffany nodded, "Well, he isn't yet, sir. I'm just afraid that this might get out of hand." He turned back to the general. "I'm not exaggerating when I say that half the agency Indians are off the reservation. And, like I said, Gatewood's scouts are acting very strange." He looked out the window, then back to the general. "At first we let them go to these dances. We just thought it was a religious thing, but the more they went the worse it got. They'd stay past their pass expiration. When they came back, they were surly and exhausted. Like they'd been on a three-day drunk." He shrugged, "It's gotten really strange, sir."

General Carr puffed on his cigarette. He glanced at the little colonel. Colonel Tibbett took his cue. "What is it you recommend, major?" he said to Tiffany, knowing what to expect. He knew Carr never made an original decision. He would ask for a consensus or solicit advice from a subordinate. If the advice was good, the victories were his. His errors were not his, simply bad advice.

Tiffany stiffened just slightly. "The first thing I recommend, sir, is to reassign all of Gatewood's scouts to Huachuca. They could go by Stevens Ranch and Solomonsville and thus avoid the agency. The population wouldn't know that we had moved them. We wouldn't tell them that they're relocating, just lead them to believe it's a normal two-day soirée." Tiffany's eyes flicked from Tibbett to the general. He knew that this was the hard part. "We could replace them with Mill's Mohaves from Company C. The Mohaves don't give a damn about this dancing business."

"What about the reservation?" Colonel Tibbett asked.

"If we are to stop the dancing, we need two more troops. We're spread too thin to hold them boys in. I thought maybe that you could request Department Command to send two down from the Bosque Redondo."

The colonel saw his chance at this. "What about the medicine man and the ones already off the reservation?"

"Gatewood's gone to talk him back."

The general sat back in his chair. Colonel Tibbet was surprised. That kind of action usually required the approval of the general. After a long moment he spoke; his voice was low, and cold and deadly. "Under whose authority, major."

"Major Redding approved it, sir." The Indian agent stiffened, his eyes finding the far wall, about six feet up, the regulation spot. His eyes focused on a single, stark nail. "But," he continued stoically, " I would have, sir, if he hadn't."

The silence was thick, like a wet cloud. Finally, the general spoke. "That'll be all, major."

As the major did a precise about-face and stepped from the room, Carr looked at his colonel. He was surprised at how angry Tibbet appeared. It made the general uncomfortable. He wondered what he had missed. He lit another cigarette to cover his confusion. "Do you think he's right?" he asked through the smoke. "To wire for two more troops."

Tibbet expected this. "They'll turn you down. It will look bad. What about the scouts?" Tibbet said, to turn the conversation.

The general took a drag. "What do you think?"

Tibbet snorted, walking over to the window. "The scouts are

soldiers. You don't molly-coddle soldiers. They're trained to obey orders."

"Yes, but they aren't white soldiers."

Tibbet turned to the general, in control now. "Edgar," he said, "There was niggers fighting on both sides at Manassas. They were soldiers just following orders. If you do special for the scouts, they'll know it and next time they'll expect more, then more after that."

The general was confused now. "Should I ask for more troops, then?" he asked.

Tibbet waved his hand, "No." He came back to the desk. He knew he had Carr now. "Give me two troops and I'll go get that pissant medicine man myself."

"What if they fight?"

Tibbet laughed, "Hell, what have they got to fight with?"

General Carr turned and stared out the window; finally he nodded. "Okay, take two troops. Which do you want?"

The little colonel smiled. "I don't care, as long as one of them is Redding's."

21

In the early hours when the dark knows what is coming and the light has not arrived, Nalin lay between wakefulness and the dreaming state where the mind is active but unencumbered. That surreal place where the mind is free to package thoughts in no logical order and the action in them becomes vivid. There is no censorship. Finally, there is a drifting sensation of floating upward toward consciousness, only to fall again.

As she fell again, her undisciplined thoughts brought the image of Chan Deisi to her. Not the man Chan Deisi, but the boy Chan Deisi. The youth of a few years ago. She dreamed of the time after her abduction, the time when her three rescuers had gained the status of heroes in the rancheria. She, on the other hand, had felt more afraid and vulnerable. If not for Gar coming along when he did, she surely would have lost her virtue and probably her life. These thoughts pushed the sleep away.

She slowly began to awaken. While still in a dreamlike state, she thought of the old days. Nalin had long been aware of the looks and attention she received from the young men. But after the abduction she felt unworthy of their attention. She was still a child and not yet a woman, so she did not understand it. She withdrew, throwing herself into the task of serving her father. But over time, there was one young man she could not ignore. She was conscious of him even in her daily chores. She found her eyes seeking Chan Deisi wherever he was.

He was different from the others. Physically he was taller, and his face was narrower, taking this from his mother. As they both grew, she could see his body forming itself into the man that would come. But it wasn't just this physical difference that drew her. It was more his calm and grounded sense of self. He did not preen and prance and show off like the other young men. Although boasting was a way of life with the others, he did not. He and his white brother were alike in this respect. They shrugged off the peer pressure to do so. Chan Deisi and Ugashe' both acted as if their prowess and skills spoke for themselves. They didn't need to bring attention to it. This was a mark of maturity that she noticed and not just her. She overheard her father speaking of it with Ochocama.

While the other boys became overly animated and, in her eyes, foolish when she and the other maidens drew near, Chan Deisi's eyes were quiet and frank and looked at her with a calm and knowing look. He rarely spoke to her, but she knew he was as aware of her as she was of him.

The thoughts were vivid now and she remembered when she was in that time of life when she was allowed very little direct contact with anyone of the opposite sex. The Dinee' society could be savage and sometimes cruel, but it was a monogamistic society that placed high value on virtue and chastity. Family was everything. Adultery was harshly dealt with among the married.

A grown man that stole the virtue of a young maiden was treated as no better than a common horse thief.

But young is young, and Nalin and Chan Deisi were young and full of life's juices. They were drawn to each other and couldn't help it. Thus, they began to dance the game that young men and women play. It began very subtly one day with an accidental and casual contact. Noch-ay-del-Klinne was visiting the lodge of Chan Deisi's grandfather and Nalin had accompanied her father. As she helped serve food to the men, her hand touched the hand of Chan Deisi. It could have been a simple and innocent touch, but it lingered longer than it should have and the jolt that ran through them was like a strike of lightening. Chan Deisi brought his eyes up and found himself submerged in the dark brown pools looking back. Engrossed in their conversation, the older men didn't notice.

Then later, Nalin was at the creek drawing water. A motion brought her head up and there on the opposite bank stood Chan Deisi quietly watching. His eyes were steady and frank. They stood silent for a long moment, then Nalin slowly untied the ribbon of cloth that held her hair. Tearing her eyes from him, she tied it to the cottonwood branch beside her. She gathered her water skin and hurried away. Later in the day she found reason to return to the creek and there where the ribbon had been tied, she found a small wooden figure of a man. A wide smile had been carved into the doll's face.

This game continued into the spring. This exchanging of small gifts became very important to the both of them. Nalin was sure everyone had to know. How could they not see the look of delicious agony that was etched on her face each time she met

Chan Deisi in the daily activities of the rancheria. A casual brush of skin, a soft-spoken word became almost more than she could bear, yet she couldn't wait for the next encounter.

Finally, the spring arrived, and the young women were off to a high mountain meadow to gather berries. As the afternoon crept on, Nalin had filled her bag and her stomach with the juicy red berries. The red stain was on her hands and mouth. She had finally turned to look for the girls, suddenly realizing that she no longer heard their voices. She found herself deep in the berry thicket very much alone.

She started working her way back through the dense underbrush and had gone only a few feet when she heard movement in the brush only a short distance away. Whatever it was, it was large. Not a rabbit. Not a squirrel. A thrill of fear ran up her back; she had no weapons and could offer little defense to a large cat or bear. The sounds came closer and closer. In a panic she cast around for a weapon. She dropped her pouch and snatched up a large stone that lay nearby. The sound now was just a few yards away. Terrified, she raised the stone over her head, poised to fight.

A voice spoke to her through the underbrush. "I seek a rabbit but find the butterfly." Chan Deisi stepped from the brush, grinning.

Nalin stood trembling, the trembling at first from fear, but now in relief and anger. She threw the stone at him. Her aim wasn't close to the target. Tears sprang to her eyes. "You frightened me!"

The grin dropped from Chan Deisi's face, and he jumped forward. "I'm sorry," he said, stricken. "I didn't mean to startle you."

She took a shuddering breath, then leaned into him as he took her forearms in his hands. She brought her face up and the trembling and tears stopped as they looked at each other. Chan Deisi was smiling again. Gently he rubbed the red stain on her face with his thumb. "Are you wounded?" he said.

"Yes," she said without a smile. This was the moment they became what they would be. Her face lifted to his, her lips slightly parted. The grin on his face slowly faded and became something else. He lowered his face and kissed her. Their eyes gently closed and with sweet slowness Chan Deisi rubbed his lips across her face. As if with one mind they sank into the warm rustling grass and with a sharp tender sweetness that almost hurt, became forever together.

22

When it became full dusk and the light was dropping rapidly from the sky, the Kid was struggling to pull his pants up. It wasn't an easy proposition, lying belly to belly and knee to knee. He had forgotten the Apaches for a while. They seemed to be gone.

"Jesus!" Molly exploded as he struggled. "Do somethin' with that belt buckle, you're about to cut me open."

"Sorry," the Kid muttered, rolling as far to his side as he could. He struggled awkwardly with this taxing situation and a fine bead of sweat popped along his upper lip. He glanced at Molly and in the dim light saw her watching his face. She was amused.

"Kid," she laughed softly, "If I didn't know better, I'd guess that you ain't used that carrot for anything much more than to pee with."

The Kid felt a flush come across his face. He was glad it was getting dark. He didn't say anything, struggling to get his belt buckled.

She chuckled, "Well?"

Embarrassed, he said, "Well what?"

"Have you?"

"Have I what?"

"You know what. Have you been with a girl before? You know, what the great unwashed say, *dipped your carrot, poked your pod*? Don't act so naïve. Have you had a woman before!"

The Kid looked at her now, suddenly angry. "Hell of a way for a woman to talk."

She stood up, catching his anger. The Apaches were forgotten. "It don't matter a good goddam if it's a woman or a man sayin' it, that's the way you boys say it!" She looked at him with scorn. "What are you? Some kinda bible thumper? Too good for a girl like me?" She brushed the pine needles out of her hair. "Jesus Christ," she said to herself. "I just had me a virgin on the side of a mountain while a pack of goddam Apaches were looking to cut my throat."

The Kid stood up, slapping the dust off of his pants. "Saltillo," he said.

"What?"

"Saltillo," he repeated. "I saw a little Mexican gal down in Saltillo a couple times."

The black-haired girl cocked her head at him, "So that's where all that experience came from," she said dryly. She turned and with a shake of her head started climbing down the rock fall.

The Kid watched her a moment, then, "Hey!" She kept moving. Again, he said, "Hey!"

She stopped and turned, glaring back up at him.

The Kid had to grin. "I love this," he said. "I just met you yesterday and you get pissed because of a gal in Saltillo and you've been with every cowboy in the Territory."

Her look was long and dark. "What you know about who I've been with wouldn't fill a pissant's watch pocket!" She started to turn away then turned back, her temper flaring, "And who I've been with and who I ain't been with ain't none of your business, and just to set the record straight, I couldn't give a goddam about you or your pokes in Saltillo!"

She turned and started back down the hill.

The Kid laughed out loud, watching her scatter loose stones in her hurry to get down the hill. He laughed again. "Hey."

Molly turned and if looks were scatterguns, the Kid would have been in pieces. "What the hell do you want?"

The Kid gestured up the hill, "The road's up this way."

She turned again, "I ain't goin' to the road."

"Where are you going."

"Back to the stage," she said over her shoulder. " I've got to find Miss Lucy's locket."

"A locket?" the Kid said, incredulously.

"Jesus Christ!" she muttered, continuing down the slide, "He's deaf."

"A locket," the Kid muttered, starting down the hill after her.

By the time the Kid reached the bottom, it was pitch dark with a hint of moon rising in the east. Molly was standing, waiting for him.

"Nice of you to wait," the Kid said dryly.

She stepped over and took his arm, smiling up sweetly at him with a sudden change of attitude. "I don't know where we are," she said.

23

It was three hours of the girl stumbling and cussing in the dark before the Kid found the spot in the wash that they had come up out of. One thing he had learned is that the girl had a vocabulary that could match any mule skinner.

The Kid had made them wait until the moon got higher and there was at least some light. After a while, working down the soft sand of the wash, the Kid got a whiff of burnt wood and charred flesh. He walked them back around the bend, where the breeze was moving away. He settled in the soft sand, leaning against the bank to wait for morning light. He pulled the girl down to sit beside him.

In the darkness, Molly leaned in against him, huddling against the cool night air. The Kid looked down at the top of her dark head and put his arms around her. He wasn't sure which emotion he was experiencing. He said softly, "Man told me once, that the quickest ride from heaven to hell and back again, would be in the arms of a woman."

"Man told you right," Molly said, eyes closed, leaning back against him, trying to sleep. After a long amount of time passed, her breathing became regular and deep. The Kid smelled the freshness of her hair. Heaven again, he mused.

At first light he roused them and started up out of the wash to where the remains of the coach lay. It was upside down, the insides charred and black. The bodies of the mutilated men and horses were buzzing with flies. The Apaches had cut chunks of meat from the hind quarters of the horses. Molly turned her head, her face pale and sick. Turning her back, she began searching the area.

The Kid looked the area over. He pointed. "We came out of the stage here and rolled down into here." Bending down Molly searched the ground for the telltale glint of silver.

"Needle in a haystack," the Kid said.

"Shut up," she said without looking up.

He looked for something to dig with. Something sharp, and hard enough to penetrate the hard ground. Then he thought of the stage. They all carried a shovel. He found it strapped to the boot. He reluctantly grabbed each of the dead men by a foot and dragged the corpses to the wash. He dug shallow graves and covered them with enough sand to keep the birds off. It wouldn't keep the scavenger coyotes away, but it would have to do until someone came from town.

He stood for a moment, watching Molly search the tobosa grass for her locket. Must be important to her, he thought. He stepped over to the upside-down coach and began rocking it, to and fro, until it finally came crashing over. The wheels were hanging over the edge of the gully, so that helped. There was still some luggage that was scattered about. Miraculously, there by the side of the road, open and scattered was Molly's valise. The package of money was there. It had been ignored. He gathered it up, walked it and the valise over to where she was still peering into the long grass. He set the valise down beside her and she barely gave it a look. She continued searching the grass. Damned odd, he thought. Looking for the locket and not concerned about the money. He half-heartedly began looking.

Finally, he said, "Maybe you could just get another one."

Without looking up she said, "It ain't mine, it's Miss Lucy's."

"Miss Lucy gave it to you?"

"No. I was taking it to Phoenix to get it cleaned."

"Can't you just get her another one?"

Molly looked up, exasperation in her eyes. "You men don't know anything." She wiped a tendril of hair away from her forehead. "This isn't just a locket. This is special. Probably an old lover gave it to her, she won't talk about it, but it must be something like that." She glanced at the Kid, "I know Miss Lucy don't care much for men, but she says it's her most prized possession."

"What was in it?" the Kid said.

"Picture of a woman," Molly said. "A young pretty woman. But she didn't look a thing like Miss Lucy. It was engraved. Said something, let me think," she put her hands to the small of her back and stretched. "I think it said something like, *Love* and a name," she paused, frowning. "I think it was Cordelia something. Cordelia Davis Page, I think."

24

The Kid looked at her sharply. "Page?"

"Do you know her?"

The Kid shook his head. "Can't say that I ever met her, but far as I know, Miss Lucy had truck with only one person named Page and that was Shonto Page."

Molly smiled suddenly, "Yes, that makes sense. He was before my time but whenever he came up, I could tell she had warm feelings for him. Picture might've been his mother or something."

The Kid's head came up and he suddenly held up his hand. "Wha..?"

"Shh," he said, interrupting her. His eyes were looking up the slope toward the eastern horizon. He froze, his eyes narrowed as he listened intently.

After a moment Molly said softly, "I don't hear. . . "

The Kid cut her off with a motion of his hand. After another long moment he suddenly reached down and hooked her valise with the same hand that held the sheathed rifle. "Time to go," he said in a low, even, voice.

He herded her ahead of him to the wash and they both

disappeared into the thick brush. Once in cover, the Kid pushed her down behind a thick, rambling creosote. After a very long time, a lone horseman appeared on the backlit horizon of the eastern slope. He was Apache, his long hair moving in the breeze. He wore an old, faded, army issue field jacket. He sat silently, studying the wrecked stage and everything around it. The Kid could hear Molly breathing and he refrained from putting a hand over her mouth.

When the man was satisfied, he turned and motioned to someone behind. A moment later the jingle of harness and the creak of leather sounded across the warm desert air. Seven other horsemen rode up beside him. These were calvary.

The Kid recognized the young soldier riding at the front. Major Redding. *The hairless one.* Called this by the scouts because he shaved daily. Too young yet to grow enough whiskers to match his counterparts.

As the squad worked its way down the slope, the Kid stepped out to greet them. He hadn't seen the major since he and John Daisy had rescued the major's young, eastern wife from Long Bedeaux at Delnorte's.

One of the other riders was in civilian clothes. It was Booker, the burley scout he had talked with at Stolvig's in Dugas. Booker rode a big sorrel that needed all its bulk to carry the man.

They came down the slope and stopped in a semi-circle around the Kid. Booker pulled his mount a little bit out and away. The young major stepped out of his saddle and taking his glove off, slapped the dust from it. He offered his hand.

"Hello, Kid," he said smiling. "You sure do show up in the damndest places."

"Major," the Kid returned, taking his hand. "How's your missus and the new baby?"

"Back east right now. Visiting her family." He turned and looked at the burned-out coach, "Looks like a helluva doin's."

The Kid turned and nodded down the wash. "I put the bodies down yonder. I imagine their kin would be happy to get them. He nodded off to the north, "Hit us from behind that bluff there, ten or twelve of them, as far as I could tell. Killed the driver and guard right off." He waved a hand back along the wash. "You'll find them not too far back. They were shot off early. I haven't buried them. Stage made it this far before they shot one of the horses and it tipped."

"Where's the others?" this from the scout, Booker.

The Kid turned his head slightly and looked up at the man. He saw that the man had positioned himself between the sun and the Kid. Here's a careful man, the Kid thought.

"I told you," The Kid said evenly. "You'll find them in the draw just like I said."

"How about you?" Booker said.

The Kid kept his eyes on the silhouetted man; he waited.

"What I mean, is," Booker continued. "How do you account for your hair still bein' in place?" It got real quiet and even the young major turned to him. Suddenly a movement from the wash turned their heads.

"I've been wondering that myself," Molly Sand said, stepping bare-legged up from the brush. "Best I can figure," she continued, stepping out in front of the astonished men, "It was clean living, moderate skill and of course, something that has

127

been his trademark so far." She looked at the young major, then to the big scout. She smiled.

"Dumb, blind luck."

In the shocked silence, the Kid said dryly. "Gentlemen, allow me to introduce Miss Molly Sand."

25

Nalin awoke with the images of her dream still with her. The sun was already in the sky. She felt as she always felt on the morning after the dancing, drained. During the daylight she felt as if she was carrying something heavy inside her and the dancing drained it away. She sat up on her pallet; it was dim inside the wickiup. She looked across to the still form of her sleeping father. As her mind went back to the previous night, she came wide awake with the memory of Chan-Deisi's arrival.

Her emotions were mixed. Pleasure that he had come. Anxiety in the fact that he carried his own beliefs. Chan-Deisi did not carry the blind faith of the other followers. Despite this, she was glad he was here. She felt more secure. She knew if there was one man among the people who could protect her father, it was Chan-Deisi.

She rubbed her eyes and face, bringing herself awake. It was warm and close inside the dwelling. She crept quietly from her bed. Taking a water skin, she left the jacale and went to the stream, moving to the place where the women relieved themselves.

She made water, but very little. Most of the moisture had

been danced from her body. Finishing, she moved across to the stream and filled the skin. She tied it off and setting it aside, she washed herself. First her face and arms and feet, then up under her cotton dress. She dropped the top of the dress and washed her arms and breasts and splashed water on her back. She wanted to completely immerse herself in the clear, cold water but she never did that unless she was with other women. Not since her abduction. Completing her toiletry, she leaned forward. Supporting herself with her hands, she lowered her face to the chill, cold water and drank deeply.

Her father was outside the lodge when she returned, sitting in his accustomed place, facing the warming sun. She did not speak to him. He preferred these moments for meditation. She quietly went about preparing the little cakes made from the ground flour of the mesquite bean that would be baked into their morning meal.

As she moved through these small, routine, and mundane tasks, she found her eyes continuing to return to her father. Looking at him. Discovering the changes that were occurring in him. He is becoming suddenly old, she thought. He had never been a big man, always physically smaller than the other men in the rancheria. Certainly, smaller than men like Chan-Deisi or Gar. Herself, even at twelve summers she had been as tall as her father and now much taller than he. But now, it seemed that he was smaller still, as if he were shrinking. His face was gaunt and tired with deep lines from his nose to his chin. The skin around his eyes was dark and deep set.

She placed a bowl of food close to his hand, but he didn't move. She knew that when he did eat, it would be sparingly, picking at it. He would have no interest in food. He sat, face to the sunlight, eyes closed. He could have been asleep.

She sat on her haunches and looked at him openly. Nalin prayed that his search would end before he just faded away. With the rising sun, the camp was awakening. There was a soft, southerly breeze and Nalin turned her face to it, enjoying the coolness before the coming of the heat of the day. She looked down the slope at the camp. It stretched randomly across the desert valley floor that was surrounded by the brilliant bursts of red rock. The high rock formations surrounded the north, east and west boundaries of the valley. The south land trailed into canyons not as brilliantly colored but still striking. They were paler where the Kaibab limestone showed through. The close, red mountains held strange and mystical shapes. This is the holy land, Nalin thought. Each time she visited it she was in awe of its majesty.

As she enjoyed the sun across her shoulders, across the valley floor she saw a band of riders coming from the southwest, moving between juniper and scrub pine. They were all men. Their ponies were painted. They were not visitors for the dance. It was a war party. They carried rifles and their ponies walked as if at the end of a long and hard journey. Nalin watched, puzzled, then she recognized the one leading. Her mouth moved in distaste. She knew him. Disalin, the cruel one. A close follower of Gar's. A beater of women and dogs.

Then Gar came into sight, striding across the open compound toward the riders. He moved easily between the wickiup clusters. People came out of their dwellings and began to gather with Gar, waiting for the riders.

Disalin slid from his pony and the two men greeted each other. Nalin was too far away to hear their voices, but she could see the body language. Disalin was very pleased with himself. Disalin lifted something small. He held it out to Gar. It glittered in the sunlight. Gar held it in his hand, studying it. He said something and Disalin nodded, turning away. He hopped back on his mount and started it toward the remuda. The other riders followed, trailing three ponies with bodies draped across them. Nalin wondered how Disalin could be happy about that. Gar turned and started up the slope toward her.

Nalin turned quickly and made herself busy. Noch-ay-del-Klinne was sitting as he had been, but when Gar's footsteps were close enough to be heard his eyes opened. He smiled. The young man came, and without formality, sat beside him. It was an act of familiarity that no one, save Nalin would have done.

Nalin moved away to give the men their privacy. The two men talked, with Gar doing the most talking. Whenever she glanced toward her father, she could tell he was not pleased with what Gar was telling him.

After a few minutes her father called to her, "Nalin." He beckoned for her to join them. She came to them and seated herself next to her father. Noch-ay-del-Klinne looked at Gar.

"I have something for you," Gar said to Nalin. He held his hand out. From it dangled a silver locket.

She didn't take it right away. In fact she didn't want a gift from Gar but her father was smiling and nodding. She reluctantly took the locket into her hand.

"It opens," Gar said.

Nalin studied the locket then unhooked the clasp. It sprung

open to reveal the likeness of a very pretty woman. She studied the inscription opposite the picture. She didn't know what it said but the indaa words must be very powerful medicine.

26

As Lieutenant Gatewood nudged his mount through the break and across the switchback moving toward the camp, his hand automatically brushed the stock of the Springfield carbine in the boot at his leg. He knew that he had been promised safety by the old chief, but the old chief was just one man. He looked across the flat in the valley below and the number of lodges were far more than he had expected.

The smell of the camp rose to him as he walked the mount closer. Smoke from the fires and dust from the many feet: it had been a dry summer and the dust rose in fine puffs with each step. He could smell the people and skins of animals stretched out to cure.

As he came into camp, the dogs came smelling at him, their rib bones showing through rangy hides. He expected them to be barking, but they didn't, just moving slowly, their curiosity dulled by hunger. There wouldn't be a jackrabbit within miles of this place. They had long been hunted out by the starving dogs. They trailed behind Gatewood for a few yards, then moved off to find a piece of shade to lie in.

The children were the same. Solemnly quiet, their eyes big in their faces, watching him. Many with hands across bloated stomachs. Most of the women had stopped to watch him. The vast majority were from the reservation, and they were dressed in shapeless cotton dresses of Mexican material.

Gatewood knew that these had been taken in raids. Most of the dresses were threadbare and worn with sewn patches on them. The men were dressed in breechclouts and knee-high moccasins. They watched him pass with sullen eyes.

The old chief was seated, cross-legged, outside his wickiup. He also was dressed in only a cloth breechclout. In the sunlight, Gatewood could see the streaks of white hair hanging to the man's shoulders, a red piece of cloth tied around his forehead. The man looks like one of the dogs, Gatewood thought. His skin was tight across his prominent ribs, but hanging loose under his eyes and at the underside of his arms. Beside the old man stood his grandson, Chan-Deisi. Gatewood was pleased to see him. John Daisy was fluent in both English and his people's language.

John Daisy stood easy; his yeller-belly Winchester casually crooked in his arm. His long dark hair was also held by a red slash of cloth, but Gatewood noted, his shirt was store bought and fairly new. He also was bare-legged with a breechclout and knee-high moccasins.

Gatewood stepped down and with a wave of Ochocama's hand, a young boy, one of the many ishikin' that were hovering around, came quickly forward and took the soldier's mount.

"You have come," the old man said.

Gatewood nodded, "As you have said."

The old man turned to John Daisy and said something, rapid

fire, that Gatewood didn't catch. He looked to John Daisy.

John Daisy smiled. He said in English, "My grandfather thinks that the Nantan Long Nose has courage; he's not as certain about your brains."

Lieutenant Gatewood looked to the old man, nodding his head. "A good

point," he smiled. "But I have orders that must be obeyed."

John Daisy translated. Ochocama shook his head, not understanding something. John Daisy explained again. Gatewood could only pick up a few words, but he got the impression that John Daisy was explaining the concept of orders.

The old chief turned to Gatewood and spoke deliberately, so that the white man could follow. "If your nantan orders you to do something, you would obey with no question?"

Gatewood nodded. "It would be my duty."

Ochocama smiled now. "This," he said, "is why the pink-faced youths can order their elders about. I have never understood that." He turned to John Daisy, shaking his head, "Dinee' will never understand these hair-faces."

He got to his feet, taking time to stretch his creaking body out. He looked around him, then down the slope. His eyes came back to the soldier with the bushy moustache and the craggy nose, and they held on him for a long moment. He held his hand out and old Nino brought him his walking stick. He nodded. "We will go see my friend, Noch-ay-del-Klinne."

He started down the slope and Gatewood and John Daisy followed. Immediately a crowd gathered, trailing behind. Gatewood was struck by the different tribes represented here.

These were not just White Mountain, but he saw Mimbre and Tontos and even some Chiricahuas and Papagos. He saw here the power of the holy man and the shadow dances. He held himself tight and controlled as he walked beside Ochocama, changing his stride to match the old man's. For the first time he realized what the army was up against. When he had left the fort, he had thought that he was going to collect an old medicine man and a few followers. He didn't think anyone at agency level was aware of the extent of this thing.

As the trio moved down the slope, toward the spring where Noch-ay-del-Klinne's lodge was located, the crowd became vocal, beginning a loud, prolonged yipping. The quick short bark of the coyote. The sound that had, for years, thrust fear into the heart of many a blue-coat soldier in the early dawn.

John Daisy watched the soldier with admiration as Gatewood ignored the growing din. He knew why Ugashe' liked this man. He would say that the man had sand. John Daisy looked off toward Noch-ay-del-Klinne's wickiup and he saw the crowd gathering there, the word having raced ahead. The people were out now and waiting.

Looking across the heads of those, his eyes found the figure of the tall girl, standing beside her father's lodge, facing toward them. Even from the distance John Daisy could feel her eyes on him.

Then from behind, moving up beside her, came Gar and the one called Disalin. These two were wearing their ghost shirts. These three disciples of Noch-ay-del-Klinne stood watching as Ochocama, the hair-face soldier and John Daisy walked up and stood before them. The noise of the people rose to an overwhelming din and Ochocama turned, suddenly angry, and raised his arm to stop it. On this cue, the noise abruptly stopped and the skin hanging at the entrance to the wickiup swung back and Noch-ay-del-Klinne stepped out.

Gatewood watched as the little man stood before Ochocama, his eyes only on his old friend. Pretending he doesn't even know I'm standing here, the soldier thought. Crafty old man, he's got control of this, and he knows it.

"You visit early, old friend," the diyin' said to the old warrior.

Ochocama nodded. "To get this done."

Noch-ay-del-Klinne's eyes swept the crowd before finally coming to rest on the tall, lanky soldier. "Yes," he murmured. "It will be best to get this done."

Ochocama indicated Gatewood with a motion of his hand. "I have promised the Nantan Long Nose that he could speak with you. I ask you to do this as a guest in my home. This hair-face is also a guest. I have agreed."

"Of course," Noch-ay-del-Klinne nodded. He turned his eyes to the tall form of John Daisy. "And who is this warrior that stands beside my old friend." He leaned forward with a smile and a mischievous glint in his eye. "He looks very familiar. I would say it was Alchesay but I know that if this is true then I must be seeing another vision!"

John Daisy laughed, along with the others close by. Nalin smiled but Gar's face remained dark. Gatewood didn't catch all of this but he saw that the small diyin' had said something amusing and the tension left the air. He could see that this was an astute man who could play people like a fiddler played a tune.

Ochocama was impatient, but he didn't want to appear so.

That would be rude. He said mildly, "It is hot standing in this sun."

Noch-ay-del-Klinne nodded. "Of course. We will go inside, out of the sun. I will send for something cool to drink." His eyes stayed on Ochocama. "Invite your hair-face friend and your grandson to join us." He turned, his eyes finding Nalin and Gar. He moved his head slightly and they immediately leaned down and stepped into the wickiup. The diyin' followed, then Ochocama and Gatewood. The last was John Daisy. As he stepped in, he caught a glimpse of the face of Disalin. It was a face filled with sheer hatred. John Daisy paused, half in and half out. He looked Disalin full in the face. He held the look, letting him know. He held his gaze for a long moment, his eyes cold and impassive, then he ducked inside.

Disalin stood staring at the skin covering the door. He suddenly realized what had been nagging him about the indaa man at the stage that had escaped with the woman.

Ugashe'!

27

Inside the dim interior of the lodge, Gatewood was surprised to see the young girl taking a seat in the circle as an equal to the men. He glanced around the circular room. It carried the heavy smoke smell that most of the lodges had. In the rising heat of the day, this made the air seem more oppressive and Gatewood could feel the sweat running down his back. Gatewood looked at the small medicine man and found the prophet looking at him. He knew there would be few pleasantries in here.

Noch-ay-del-Klinne got right to it, "My old friend has asked me to hear your message. I am listening."

Gatewood looked to John Daisy. "It will be easier if you translate." John Daisy nodded. The lieutenant spoke slowly, feeling his words out, his voice controlled and strong. "Since the time of Nantan Crook, the chief you call *Gray Wolf*, it has been decided that all the people are to stay on the land that the great father in Washington has set aside for them. By leaving the reservation without permission and by allowing your people to follow, you have broken this agreement." He glanced at John Daisy and the young man repeated his words.

Gar snorted, "Agreement? What agreement? We stay where it is impossible to live and you agree not to shoot us?"

Noch-ay-del-Klinne held up his hand for silence. Gar swallowed his anger and was silent. John Daisy didn't translate this, he just nodded to Gatewood. Gatewood continued, "Out of respect for my friend Ochocama, I have come alone to bring you the words of the nantan of the soldiers fort." He leaned slightly forward, "I could have come with many soldiers and guns. But I did not. I did not because I have heard that Noch-ay-del-Klinne is a man of peace. A wise man. I know that he was among those that visited the far away city of the great father of all the white nation. He has seen the power of this nantan."

When John Daisy repeated this, Noch-ay-del-Klinne inclined his head acknowledging this fact. He remembered that trip well. He also remembered that when he had returned and told of the wondrous things he had witnessed, many had turned their backs to him, choosing not to believe.

Gatewood continued, "On this very day, you must return to the agency or the nantan of the fort will order me to bring many guns against you and take you back by force. This, I do not wish to do, for I fear many will be killed." He paused and looked from Noch-ay-del-Klinne to Ochocama and back. He continued, "However, if I am ordered to do this, it will be done."

Gar's face twisted with anger, "Large words for one that sits alone."

John Daisy looked at the scarred man. "He does not sit alone."

"You would side with this hair-face against your own people?" Gar snarled.

Nalin spoke for the first time. "Chan-Deisi sides with his

grandfather. This soldier is a guest of Ochocama and will be treated with respect. He has promised Nantan Gatewood safety and it will be so."

Ochocama sat silent. Nalin turned to her father, "What will we do?"

Noch-ay-del-Klinne took his eyes from Gatewood and never looked at him again. He turned to John Daisy, "Tell the hair-face that Noch-ay-del-Klinne is very tired, and it will take me time to rest and be ready. Tell him that I will return in three days."

Gar started to protest but Noch-ay-del-Klinne held up his hand to silence him. "Tell him that," he said to John Daisy but looking at Gar.

John Daisy repeated what the diyin' had said. Gatewood sat for a long moment thinking. It would take three days to muster a force into the field and travel here anyway. He nodded, getting to his feet, "Three days."

John Daisy stood also to follow the soldier, for his safety more than anything

Ochocama stood, signifying the end of the meeting. He was relieved that this was done. Gatewood stood aside and the old man left the lodge, the white soldier right behind. John Daisy followed Gatewood and as he stepped through the entrance he glanced back. Gar was looking at Noch-ay-del-Klinne, a small smile on his face. Nalin's eyes were also on her father and for the first time, John Daisy noticed a small silver locket resting in the hollow of her throat. Nalin was not smiling. Her eyes were solemn and troubled. It was then that John Daisy knew for certain what he had known all along. Noch-ay-del-Klinne had no intention of going back to San Carlos.

28

John Daisy rode with Gatewood until he was satisfied the soldier was safe. Noch-ay-del-Klinne lay on his pallet, still tired from the dances. Ochocama went back to his lodge to rest and Nalin took a basket up the western slope to search for chokeberries and mesquite beans. This is where Gar found her.

This pleased Gar that she was alone. He hailed her and she straightened then without returning his greeting; she waited for him to come near. She smoothed her dress against her legs as she waited. He was the last one she wanted to see.

"We must talk," he said as he strode up.

"There has already been much talk," she said off-handedly.

"Exactly!" he spat. "Too much talk. That is all there is! Talk, talk, talk! When is your father going to do more than talk?"

"Why don't you ask him?" she answered.

Gar was suddenly angry. "I have," he said coldly. "He puts me off. He only says that we must wait until all things are right."

"Then that is what we must do."

"That is all we have been doing. It has gone beyond that now."

He took a sudden breath and held it, getting control of his anger. He let the air out slowly then said, "We have been waiting for many months. We are finished with waiting. The waiting time is over. Noch-ay-del-Klinne wants to move away, to run from the hair- face.

"Not to run away," Nalin interrupted. "He wants to go to the holy ground, to gather our people around us. To be safe."

"And then what?"

Nalin looked down and across the valley at the many lodges scattered there. She turned and looked at Gar. "As I said, to be safe."

"We will never be safe from the blue-coat soldiers. Not until we rise up and take care of them. You and your father don't know anything, but I know."

Nalin stepped away and swept him with a challenging look. "Just what does the great Gar know?"

He reached out and grabbed her arm, his fingers digging into her skin. "Do not mock me, girl." He pulled her roughly closer, his eyes fierce now. "Your father is no warrior, and you are no warrior. I am the one that must lead our people! My warriors are ready to act now. They will not wait much longer."

She struggled to pull from his grasp, her face flushed with anger, but his grip was too strong. Now he had both her arms and had pulled her harshly into him. "This is what must be done. You are a diyin', I am the warrior. Together we must lead the people against our enemies and drive them from our land. With Nalin and Gar together, all the people will follow, even the weak old women of Ochocama's camp."

Nalin struggled with him, but he was much too powerful. He

released one arm and slid his arm around her. He pressed himself hard against her and she could feel his manhood against her belly. "We will go to your father and tell him that we wish to be as one. I will bring you into my lodge."

"I will not be your woman," she managed, pushing against him.

His mouth was on her now. "Don't you see," he breathed. "It is the only way. We must be the ones that save our people."

Shock and surprise gave way to fierce anger. Arching her back she spat, "I would rather mate a dog!" She swung her free hand and it cracked against his face.

Gar became very still, and they stood pressed together for a long moment, then he released her. His eyes were dark and murderous. They stood just a foot apart. Gar's mouth turned up in a snarl and he said with deep contempt, "You are not worthy." His face was twisted now, and she turned to bolt but he grabbed her dress and swung her around. With clenched fist he clubbed her twice against the side of her head. The sound was a sick and meaty sound. Like kicking a side of beef. She fell to the ground dazed. He stood over her then deliberately pulled his foot back and kicked her in the stomach. Her breath exploded from her lungs, and she rolled over gasping for air.

"Now who is the dog?" Gar snarled.

She heard him as he walked away. She lay for a long time in agony, barely able to breathe. She knew one thing. No one should know. Especially Chan Deisi.

29

Molly sat to the side, atop a large slab of granite, with one leg cocked up, inspecting her sore and bruised foot. She was seemingly unaware of the commotion her exposed thigh and ankle was causing in the ranks.

There were close to a hundred calvary milling about now. Major Redding's squad had been closely followed by troops C and D, commanded by Colonel Tibbet. Molly thought the pink faced major was kinda cute but took one look at the diminutive, stiff demeanor of the colonel and immediately wrote him off as a prig. She turned and while pretending to be self-engrossed, she was secretly watching the Kid.

The major had ordered one of the troopers to give her a blanket, but the morning was warming, and the blanket lay in a discarded heap beside her. She knew that the Kid was aware of the commotion her bare leg was causing, and it seemed to amuse him. This irritated her.

The Kid had been in a long discussion with the young major and the young officer had called for a saddled horse for him. Now the Kid walked across to Molly, reins in his hand. He looked like he was ready to travel.

Molly looked down at him. "You're fired," she said.

The Kid laughed. "You didn't hire me."

"Well, take a good look, because it's me that's firing you."

The Kid was suddenly solemn. "It don't matter," he said. "I can't go on anyway, the major's gonna get you to Yarnell and on the Phoenix stage."

"Miss Lucy hired you to get me to Phoenix!"

"You'll have an Army escort and besides, I thought you just fired me," the Kid smiled.

Molly ignored this, "Where are you goin' that's more important?"

The Kid turned casually, looking to see who was in earshot. He turned back to Molly and dropped his voice. "Major Redding," he said nodding toward the young officer, "told me that the little pissant there," he said, indicating the colonel," has orders to kill a friend of mine."

"What friend?"

The Kid shrugged. "It's a long story. Needless to say, the little jerk is doing it for the glory of killing Indians. Tell Miss Lucy I apologize, but I don't have a choice."

"Miss Lucy said you were raised by the Apache?"

The Kid looked at her for a long moment. He stepped up into the saddle. "I have friends and relatives this guy wants to kill. I have to go. I'll explain to Miss Lucy when I get back."

Molly slid down from her perch and put a hand onto his leg. "Kid," she said. "I've gotta get that locket back."

The Kid looked into her slate grey eyes. He nodded, "Yeah, I figured that out. I reckon since we didn't find it, one of those that hit the stage picked it up and if I'm guessing right, that locket's headed to the same place I am. I'll look for it when I get there."

He nudged the horse and started away.

"Good luck, Kid," she said softly. "Look for the locket."

He walked the borrowed mount a few steps, then turning to look back, he saw that Molly was still standing there watching him. He swung the mount around and rode back to her. Before she could react, he reached down and swung her off the ground and up to him. He kissed her. He set her back down, grinning, "You wanna know something?" he said, turning the horse.

"What?" she answered, flustered.

"I never knew any Mex gal in Saltillo," he laughed, kicking the brown away and up the slope.

30

In the early morning hours before the sky was light, Nalin rose and slid silently out of the lodge. She moved gingerly, sore from the beating. She wound her way through the silent wickiups. It was still dark with only a hint of light in the eastern sky and a sliver of moon to light her surroundings. She knew the path well and moved steadily.

She found Chan Deisi where she knew she would. He was in the higher ground, by the massive red rock butte that was just beginning to glow orange in the coming light. He sat cross-legged, wearing only a breechclout, facing the growing light. He was on a large flat boulder that jutted angrily from the rock wall with nothing but a hundred feet of air under it. Nalin made no attempt to conceal her footsteps.

He heard her approach and stood, turning to her. She walked to him, and her voice was soft in the dark.

"Hold me," she said.

His arms opened and he held her. There were no words that could express what the holding did. They stood like this for a very long time. They watched as the morning light crept across the valley floor below, the darkness lifting back from the ground like a shadowed blanket.

Suddenly, the ache in Nalin welled and tears wetted her cheeks. Chan Deisi leaned down, pressing his lips against them. He tightened his grip and felt her wince. "What is it?" he asked.

She shook her head. "Nothing," she said, "I tripped and fell while gathering berries." She squeezed him as hard as her strength allowed, feeling the broad slabs of muscle in his back and shoulders. He stroked her thick, black hair.

When she could trust herself to speak, she said, "This is where I belong. With these arms around me."

After a moment, he said softly, "I could not live on a reservation. In captivity."

She nodded, leaning her cheek against his shoulder. "I would die gladly to return the land to our people. But the land will never again belong to us."

Nalin looked up at him.

"The whites are like ants," he continued. "You can destroy the entire hill but they will be back, and in numbers greater than before."

"My father has seen the vision," Nalin said.

"Yes, the vision," he said.

She pulled slightly away from him. "You do not believe in the spirits." It was more statement than question.

Chan Deisi shrugged. "I have seen and heard much. I have listened to the Nakaiye' Padre and he told me of his spirits. Ugashe' has told me of the white man's spirits." He looked into her eyes with a slight smile. "And now Noch-ay-del-Klinne tells me of his spirits. I do not know what spirits are true."

"Come be with me. Our people need you."

He laughed without mirth. "The people don't need me. They have your father and the great warrior Gar." He felt her tremble. "What is it?"

"Gar would lead the People to war."

"Gar is a fool."

"Yes," she agreed. "But the warriors need someone to follow, and they follow him." She suddenly reached up and kissed him. "They would follow you if you would lead."

He laughed again. "Follow me where?"

"I am serious," she said. "They would follow you to the Madres. The Nakaiye' are weak. We could live there."

"All the People?"

She shrugged. "I don't know, but it is better than where we go now."

The light was full now and Chan Deisi brushed a tendril of hair back away from her face. "To the Cibicue."

She nodded slightly, her cheek rubbing his shoulder. "Yes, my father will dance there."

"If General Carr allows it."

She looked up into his eyes. "That is why I need you there. I need you with me." She kissed him again, holding the promise of her body against him. "Please come with me."

"I must find Ugashe', then I will come," he said.

"Yes, always Ugashe'," she said. She sank to the ground pulling him down. "Hurry," she said breathlessly, "My father will be looking for me."

31

When the sun was fully up, Gar urged his bony mount into the water and across the rocky bottom of Carrizo Creek. The waters of the creek came sluicing down through the break in the canyon and ran, at its deepest, knee high across the smooth, rounded stones that covered the bottom. His pony was skittish and nervous, not finding solid footing in the water. Ahead of him, across the sandy flood plain, he could see Nalin packing the old horse she rode, getting ready for the day's travel to Cibicue.

Noch-ay-del-Klinne sat in the shade of a cottonwood, smoking. It had been two days since they had left Ochocama's rancheria. The gathering there had dispersed into many smaller bands and scattered through the mountains. They were all headed to Cibicue.

A small handful of Gar's closest followers traveled with him, the diyin' and the girl. Watching Nalin move around the camp, Gar felt the anger in his belly, an anger fired by rejection. She had not spoken to him since the leaving and Noch-ay-del-Klinne had been almost utterly silent. This was the last of the three days that the hair-face, Nantan Long Nose, had given him to return to San Carlos and Gar knew that this weighed heavily on the old man.

Gar kneed his pony and walked it along the creek toward the tree line, away from the diyin' and Nalin. He was afraid to be too close this morning. He was afraid that the little diyin' would look at him and see his thoughts.

He had awakened this morning and he knew that what he had come to believe was true. The diyin' would not have the strength and courage to fulfill their destiny. Gar knew the old man would buckle under the pressure of the hair-face soldiers and then the spirits would not rise to fight. For the first time, his faith was shaken in Noch-ay-del-Klinne.

Gar had awakened this morning knowing that he, alone, should wear the mantle of leadership. That it was up to him to rally his spirit shirt warriors and to call upon *those that went before* and drive the whites from Dinee' land.

In the long shadow of a grove of cottonwoods, lining the far side of the creek bottom, Gar glimpsed a shadowy movement. Two riders worked their way out of the dark underbrush and moved toward him.

One was Disalin, the other a Mimbrenos scout that Gar knew by his Nakaiye' name, *Bonito*. Bonito had been a scout and wore the faded blue field jacket that had been given to him by the hair-face soldiers.

Gar moved his pony to a level spot well out of earshot of Nalin or her father. He waited for the two men to cross the creek and work their way to him. There had been a time that Gar had hated all that rode as scouts for the hair-faces. But now he found that they ranked among his strongest supporters of the dances.

Disalin spoke as they drew close, "This one has come from San Carlos. He has something to tell Noch-ay-del-Klinne."

Gar nodded to the man. "It is good for Bonito to join us. I am Gar. Tell me what you have to say." Bonito was uncertain. He glanced at Disalin.

Disalin nodded. "Tell him."

Bonito said, "The Nantan Tibbet with the young Nantan Redding comes to Cibicue with over three hundred troops. They will take Noch-ay-del-Klinne there. It is said that they will kill him."

"Who says?" Gar asked.

Bonito shrugged, "One of the hair-face soldiers. He was drunk on tizwin. He was trying to rid himself of his insides. I helped him. He said that I was soon to be a *good injun*. He said the diyin' would soon be a good injun too."

"What does that mean, good injun?"

Bonito looked at the scarred man. "Some hair-face say that a good injun is a dead injun."

"When do they come?" Gar asked.

Bonito shrugged, "They are riding now." He glanced again at Disalin. "We must warn Noch-ay-del-Klinne not to go to Cibicue."

Gar held up his hand. "I will talk with him, but I know that he will go on. Do not mention this again."

Bonito looked at the man, then with another slight shrug said, "I have done what I will do." He urged his pony around and walked it away.

Disalin swung his pony around, "There is something else."

Gar waited.

Disalin took a moment, then, "I told you of the man and the woman that escaped from us when we hit the hair-face stage."

"That disappeared into the desert," Gar said coldly.

Disalin went on, "There was something about the man that has been bothering me. Something vaguely familiar. I only got a glimpse, and then they disappeared."

"What is it?" Gar said impatiently.

"When I saw Chan Deisi, I wondered where Ugashe' was, then I realized, the man was Ugashe'."

"Ugashe'?"

Gar sat silently for a moment. He turned to Disalin, his eyes slits of hatred. "Ugashe' will come to Chan Deisi and they will try to talk the girl and her father into surrender. Take Bonito and your best men and wait for them. Go to the canyon and wait for them there. It is the way they will come. They must be stopped."

32

The land that spread itself between the Yarnell road and the red rock canyons was a harsh and empty land, littered with the high buttes and jutting castles of limestone covered with scrub brush. The sky over this land was an endless sky and the openness seemed forever. This land was rimmed by a vast walled jumble of stone and cactus. The trail from east to west could only breech this wall in just a few places. This was why the Kid was able to find John Daisy sitting in a clump of junipers.

They spotted each other from a quarter mile away and John Daisy sat easy in the shade, cross-legged on the ground while the big appaloosa was munching nearby. The Kid finally drew up and he swung down with a grin. "You lost?"

"Just waiting on you," John Daisy returned.

The sun was high, and the Kid took a pull on his canteen and passed it to John Daisy. He dug a can of peaches from his possible bag and opened it with the knife from his knee-high moccasin. The two men shared it while they listened to each other's stories. When the last of the sweet juice was gone, the Kid tossed the can aside.

"Tibbet is a popinjay. He will kill Nalin and her father for the slightest reason. He thinks he'll be a hero. He knows that after Custer the nation is looking for a hero."

John Daisy said, "Noch-ay-del-Klinne will not run. He will be at Cibicue."

"So will we," the Kid said.

John Daisy shrugged and stepped up on the appaloosa. He had known that they never had a choice.

Over the valley and up the eastern slope to the far purple mountains was a long hard climb. Once out of the red rock canyons, much of the ground was almost impassable, consisting of jumbled boulders, sharp rocks and deep ravines. Because of the switchbacks and impassable ground, a rider would have to travel three or four miles to achieve only one. This was Dinee' land. A land that could hide a small band easily. After half a day the young white man and his Indian brother broke out of the rough country and faced a long sloping rise that went for miles. Eventually it reached the tall pines that separated one part of the territory from the other.

The Kid felt lucky that the whiskerless major had loaned him his personal second mount. He knew the major felt he owed the Kid and John Daisy a debt for saving his pregnant wife's life from Long Bedeaux. The major knew good horse flesh. He was thankful that the major had not given him just any mount from the remuda. This one was a rugged mountain pony, with grit and staying power. The brown was staying with the appaloosa and that was saying something. John Daisy and the appaloosa looked as if they were out for a Sunday stroll.

The two men rode cautiously, the Kid with his Walker Colt

limber in his belly holster and John Daisy with his Winchester lying across the neck of the big spotted mare. They finally had to stop when it became too dark to continue. They made a dry camp, ate a little then rolled into their blankets early. They were moving again at the first hint of light.

They finally reached the high craggy mountains that had loomed for so long in front of them. The air was filled with the sweetness of pine needles instead of the dust of the valley floor. The traveling got rough again and they urged their ponies on. Up ahead there appeared an impenetrable wall of mountains. A stranger would make many false starts to find the pass that led to the land beyond. John Daisy and the Kid knew this land. They knew the pass where the waters started that became Carrizo Creek. They knew the pass that would lead them through the ragged canyons and out the other side to the sloping hills at Cibicue.

A good place for careful, the Kid thought, as they started up the trail that followed the canyon wall. It was rough going, the trail moving up at a steep angle, following the twisting breaks and cuts in the wall of rock. At times the trail was as wide as fifteen feet, other times it was barely enough for four hoofs to fit. Again, the Kid silently thanked the major for picking a sure-footed pony.

Up on the side of the canyon, as they climbed, they tried to move as quickly as possible, not liking to be exposed. Their eyes were busy, watching the trail ahead and the turns coming up, and the canyon wall only a couple hundred feet across dead air. The Kid was leading, his pony not moving as fast as the appaloosa wanted to.

Just ahead, before the next turn, was a large sumac growing in a lonely spot in the middle of the trail. The path split around it, wider to the outside. Beside it, just before the turn, there was a split in the canyon wall that ran straight up. The split left an area like a roofless chimney just behind the sumac. The trail disappeared around the turn, but across the sixty yards of air it was visible again. There was a jumble of fallen rock there.

Not really thinking why, the Kid reined his mount to the inside of the sumac instead of to the easier, wider trail to the outside. As he passed under the tree, his pony reared its head to avoid a lower branch. There was a sudden shot and a puff of smoke from the fallen rock across the chasm. The bullet caught the brown in the underside of his neck, just in front of its intended target, the Kid's chest. The horse screamed and reared backwards with the startled Kid doing his best to kick himself free.

33

As the horse went backwards, ass over teakettle, it flashed through the Kid's mind that he had three options. Kick away hard and go over the edge, just slide off the dying horse and let it land seven hundred pounds of animal on him, or just get dumb lucky.

He did it just right, kicking himself free, right into a rock the size of a buffalo's head. He cracked his head so hard that blood flew. Momentum rolled him behind the rock and to the edge of the cliff and he lay face down, dazed, looking stupidly at his numb hand clutching the Walker Colt. It seemed like it took him about a day to turn his head and look at the major's pony. It lay on its side, quivering, hind-legs just in front of him. Its eyes were staring, and blood was pumping from the wound. The shot must have hit the jugular.

The Kid's whole body was buzzing from the blow, but he managed to turn his head and look at John Daisy. At the shot, John Daisy had stepped the appaloosa into the split in the rock and he had her backed up against the ledge. He was down off her, his Winchester ready. He was looking at the Kid, grinning.

John Daisy had a quirk that irritated the Kid. The worse things were, the bigger his grin.

"Damn fool," the Kid said aloud, only it came out sounding like "Duufoof!"

The Kid shook his head and the ringing in his ears diminished somewhat. It was replaced by the sound of gunfire. He was behind the rock he'd cracked his head on, but he realized that it was only sheltering his front half. His butt and legs were hanging out into the open. As he looked back at them, sudden puffs of dust exploded close to his left thigh. It dawned on him that the worst fate that could befall a man, beside making a fool of himself with a woman, was to find himself shot in the butt.

The Kid gathered himself, then rolled toward John Daisy. One of the Apaches took a lucky last shot and hit a chunk of quartz next to his head and it spit a spray of dirt and rock into his face. He rolled into John Daisy's legs, spitting dirt. He looked up at his Indian brother.

"Quite a party, ain't it?" John Daisy said, still smiling.

While the Kid struggled to sit up, John Daisy snaked the barrel of his Winchester around the side of the split and fired three quick left-handed rounds. There was no way to take an aim without stepping out, he just wanted to show the ambushers that he was still there.

The Kid scooted up next to the rock, fingering the lumpy, sticky spot at the top of his head. He looked around. They were well hidden for the time being, but they couldn't go forward or backward without giving the ambushers a clear shot. He looked across the canyon, then to John Daisy.

John Daisy shrugged, thinking the same thought. Eventually

one of those men on the other side would realize that if their best shot made its way across the canyon, he'd have a clear hundred and fifty yard shot at an open target.

John Daisy squatted down and looked at the Kid. The appaloosa stood quietly beside him, her ears up. The Kid checked the loads in the Walker Colt, then slipped the thong on his hip pistol and checked it. John Daisy was still smiling. That was his way, the tougher it got, the smilier he was.

Looking around, the Kid figured that John Daisy oughta be happier than hell before this was over. Of course, the Kid knew that as long as John Daisy was smiling, he was okay, it was the other guys that should be worried.

"Well, shik'isn," the Kid said. "Got any ideas?"

John Daisy thumbed three shells into the Winchester. He turned and looked across the canyon. The red bandana tied around his head was dark with sweat. His features were more angular than most Apaches.

"Maybe they'll surrender," he said. His eyes caught a circling hawk, and the Kid lifted his head to look at it.

"My grandmother told me that her mother had learned to fly. Was taught by a giant crow that she had caught. Could just jump up into the air and fly away," John Daisy said, eyes twinkling. "Maybe that's what we will do, just fly away."

"Fly like a rock," the Kid said.

There was another shot, and splinters of rock showered them. The appaloosa moved nervously. The Kid climbed to his feet, staying back in the recession. He looked all around, thinking. He finally looked up and saw their chance. Above their heads was a vertical fissure in the rock. A chimney that had split straight up.

The Kid thought it was big enough for a man to edge his way to the top.

The Kid unbuckled his gun belt and slung it over his shoulder. John Daisy was looking up at the fissure. It didn't start for a good eight feet above their heads. The rock around it was smooth, with no handholds

"How are you gonna get started up there?" John Daisy asked.

The Kid nodded at the big mare. "I'll stand on her."

John Daisy took the appaloosa's bridle and held her steady while the Kid climbed on top. He carefully stood on her back, his hands against the face of the cliff for support. There were two more shots that screamed off the bare rock but the horse stood still, like she knew what John Daisy wanted. The beginning crack of the chimney was now waist-high on the Kid. He could just get his foot into it. He would have to lunge forward, putting a hand inside each edge of the crack then press outward to hold himself in place. The pressure alone would have to keep him balanced; there was nothing to grasp.

Across the way, the firing continued sporadically.

"Here goes nothin," the Kid muttered and pushed off the appaloosa's back. His foot wedged tight and he found himself standing upright, face into the rock, straining against the sides to hold himself in place. The pressure on his foot was tremendous and he was afraid that he'd wedge his foot so hard that he wouldn't be able to get it out again.

He turned his head, straining to look upward. His cheek was against the wall, and he couldn't see well, not daring to push away from the cliff for a better look. He turned his head around and looked down. There was a very small outcropping of ledge just above knee high. Hoping it would hold, he brought his free foot up and stepped up on it. At the same time his hands reached up to new pressure points. The chimney was wider here.

He felt that his shoulders were about to come out of the sockets. Now the chimney was getting wider, and he could bring a knee up against the wall and place his shoulder against the other side. By pushing his knees against one side and his shoulder against the other, he could take the pressure off his hands. He stayed like that a moment giving his hands and arms a rest.

After a short rest, he began inching his way up the fissure, knees against one side, back and shoulders against the other. Nearing the top, a scraping noise below him caught his attention. He paused, then threw a cautious glance below. John Daisy had started up, his Winchester hanging from his back. Below him, the appaloosa fidgeted, tied to a small creosote that was growing from a crack in the wall.

The firing had virtually stopped now, and the Kid knew that this meant that they had finally sent at least one man across the canyon for a clear shot. He worked harder now, pushing his way up. After an eternity, he finally rolled over the top. He kept rolling several feet away from the edge before sitting up. He lifted the pistol belt over his head and checked the loads.

Suddenly John Daisy's voice came echoing up over the edge. "Ugashe'!" His voice was urgent. "Ugashe'," he called again. The Kid crawled back to the edge, a pistol in each hand. He cautiously peered over the side. John Daisy was within ten feet of the top, but his head was twisted around, and he was looking back across the canyon. The Kid followed his line of sight.

Only two hundred yards away, Disalin stood across the

canyon. He was up on a big slab of granite, legs spread for balance. He was aiming down the sights on his rifle, and he had John Daisy hanging out on the side of the cliff.

34

The scout's Coyotero name was Tloh-ka. To pronounce it properly you had to hold your tongue just right and, with a low guttural sound, let the name roll out of your throat. The white troopers had no patience for this and so they called him Dandy Jim. He had begun as a scout, eight years previously, with the Dandy Fifth and he was Dandy Jim from then on.

He had spent the last two days, along with Mose and the other scouts, ranging two or three miles in front of the column. There had been plenty of sign and he had told the Nantan Long Nose that it was obvious that the gathering at Ochocama's had scattered, but they were all headed to the same place. To the Cibicue. He knew that the diyin' would dance again at the Cibicue.

The Nantan Long Nose had agreed and had told the little nantan, Tibbet. Now the column was headed straight for the pass at Carrizo Creek. Dandy Jim rode easy, with the other scouts, and wondered what would happen when they reached the camp of Noch-ay-del-Klinne. He and the other scouts had never really mingled with the soldiers but over the years there had been a mutual trust and respect between them. Now, that was changed. The scouts kept to themselves, even camping out and away from the main camp at night. The soldiers had begun looking at them with distrust and, even at times, with open hostility. Only Gatewood had not changed, but Dandy Jim knew that Gatewood was aware of the feelings. He had to be. Several of the scouts, including Bonito, had simply disappeared.

The second night out, as the light began to fade, each trooper went about his assigned task, as was custom, at Gatewood's order, Sergeant Barnes selected a scout to picket the horses, and stand watch through the night. This night he selected Dandy Jim.

As light broke on the morning of the third day, Gatewood was aroused by a loud stream of invectives that only a career soldier would know. He rolled out of his blankets and walked swiftly to where Sergeant Barnes was loudly berating someone. Once he was over the surprise awakening, Gatewood had to almost smile. Someone was really catching hell. And, with language so profane and colorful that it was almost poetic.

Halfway across the now awake camp, Gatewood met Sergeant Barnes on his way back from the rocky area of the horse picket. The veteran was still muttering to himself.

"What is it, sergeant?"

"What in the hell is going on here?" Colonel Tibbet came striding up, buttoning his normally immaculate blouse.

The sergeant was so mad he was still sputtering. He was shaking his head. "He must have shit for brains. He looked at Gatewood, exasperated. "It's Dandy Jim, sir."

"Dandy Jim?" Colonel Tibbet said, looking to Gatewood.

"One of the scouts," Gatewood explained. He nodded to the sergeant,

"Go ahead."

The older sergeant took a breath, "He was the one that I had on picket last night."

"Did he take off?" Gatewood asked.

Barnes shook his head, "No, not that, sir. He's still here but he had half the mounts picketed in that grove of palo verdes." He was shaking his head in disgust.

Tibbet looked at Gatewood, beginning to be irritated. "Lieutenant, tell me what the hell he is talking about."

"Our scout picketed the mounts in the palo verde trees, sir," Gatewood explained. "There's not much grass in there, so the horses will eat the bark."

The colonel just looked at him, still puzzled.

"It makes them sick, sir."

"Yessir," Barnes spoke up. "Gives them a mean belly ache, and makes 'em shit big green puddles! Ain't no way we will be able to make the pace we did yesterday."

Tibbet was livid. "I want that man on report and I want him disciplined when we return to the fort, lieutenant!"

"Yessir," Gatewood responded.

Tibbet turned, looking eastward, hands on his hips. "How much time will we lose?"

"Maybe half a day if they aren't too bad."

"Dammit!" Tibbet exploded. "I wanted to force march into Cibicue today. Catch the bastard in the afternoon light. Now we'll have to stop at Carrizo, go in tomorrow." He turned to Gatewood, his eyes slits, his voice shaking with anger. "When we get back, I'll have that red nigger's ears!" He turned and stalked away.

Gatewood looked at Barnes, then turned and looked back at the horse picket. Dandy Jim stood off to the side, looking back up at him. Their eyes met and Dandy Jim's didn't waver.

"Bastard meant to do it," Gatewood said.

35

Disalin's first shot was low. It hit with a smack, then went screaming down the canyon. John Daisy was working his way upward as fast as he could. The Kid had a pistol in each hand, but they didn't have the range. His rifle was still in the beaded case, strapped to his dead horse. He fired twice, hoping to distract Disalin, but it didn't help,

Disalin's next shot was closer and to the side. The Kid unstrapped his gun belt and lying flat, dropped it over the side, holding one end. John Daisy reached high and got a hand on it.

Disalin's next shot spit chunks of dirt in John Daisy's face. He wasn't grinning now. The Kid pulled with all his might and John Daisy walked up the chimney and scrambled over the edge as Disalin unloaded several shots.

John Daisy came up over the edge and fell across the Kid. They struggled back away from the edge and lay there panting. John Daisy looked over at the Kid and the grin was back.

The Kid sat up rubbing his leg. He'd barked his shin and the lump on his head was throbbing. He spit out some grit. "How many are there?" he asked.

John Daisy shrugged, swinging his Winchester around, levering a round into the chamber. "I thought you were counting," he said.

The Kid spit again, exasperated. "Well, shit, we don't even know how many there are or where they are exactly."

"I know where one of them is," John Daisy said, crawling back toward the edge. "And it looks like he's headed back this way."

"Did you see who it was?"

John Daisy glanced back to the Kid. He nodded. "Yeah, I saw."

The Kid crawled up beside him, peering over the edge. "Do you think he knows who he's shootin' at?"

John Daisy smiled, "Oh yeah, he knows."

He handed the Kid the Winchester, "Count'm," he said. With that he jumped up and started barking like a coyote. He turned his back and started slapping his buttocks in the classic Apache insult.

Groaning, the Kid rolled to his side and slid the barrel of the rifle over the edge pointing it at the other side of the canyon. Four incensed Apaches came up and started firing at the fool. The Kid was ready and levered three quick rounds. They dropped back to cover. One of them went down awkwardly and the Kid thought, maybe, he'd hit him.

John Daisy jumped back down. "How many?"

The Kid shook his head in disgust, "Was four, maybe three now." He handed the Winchester back and John Daisy thumbed three new cartridges in.

"What now, ass slapper?" the Kid said.

"Well, I ain't goin' back down that cliff," John Daisy stated, moving away from the edge. "I guess we'll go visit this dog *chaa'*."

"Hooray," the Kid said getting to his feet and following him. They scrambled back down the other side of the slope. It was very rocky. They were kicking up dust and loose shale. John Daisy kept them on a course that would bring them around behind Disalin and the rest.

Once they got to even ground, they began to move faster. The Kid figured that the Apaches would try the same flanking movement and so now it was a foot race. As young boys living in a lizard hard desert, moving rapidly across this kind of terrain was like a city kid playing in a park. There were many games of childhood and in the rancheria most of these games had sprung from a basis of survival. Many of the games were grueling contests that tested not only a boy's flesh but his will and stamina.

One of these games was to fill your mouth with water then run two miles up a mountain slope and back. Four miles in the high desert sun. The achievement was in spitting the water at the feet of your opponent at the end of the race.

Many of the games were contests of cunning and skill. These could be against an opponent or a team of opponents. These were games that taught the young boys the skills that they would need later. Skills that included tracking and hunting and eluding pursuers and hiding in all terrain even when there was no cover. These games were encouraged by the elders.

One such game was of the wolf and the fox. The fox carried a piece of cloth tied around his arm and he would disappear into the desert. The wolf pack must find him and retrieve the cloth without being ambushed, for even the fox has sharp teeth. This taught not only stealth and concealment, but also, how to track a dangerous prey.

The Kid had already been an accomplished tracker when he came to live with John Daisy, having been taught by Shonto Page. But the art of concealment was another thing.

Most all of the warriors in the rancheria were accomplished at concealment, but in Ochocama's rancheria there was a legendary warrior that was known as Tatsah'dasaygo, *the Quick Killer*. This one had served as scout for General Crook, and no one was better at concealment. It was told that he had once challenged the general to find him after the general turned his back for a few short seconds. They had stood in a wide-open place with no cover for many yards. The general complied and when he turned back, the old warrior was gone. Simply disappeared without enough time to reach cover. It was told that the general searched for five minutes before a fiendish apparition rose suddenly from the ground not an arm's length from the general.

It was a great joke and was told many times around the fires of the rancheria. It was this one that John Daisy and his white brother, Ugashe' sought out. If they were to be taught, they would be taught by the best.

John Daisy set a quick pace across the broken ground, and they were moving fast and hard toward the attackers. The Kid knew that John Daisy was figuring on the ambushers to be moving just as quickly, coming after them, not figuring that their prey would be heading toward them. It took a while for the two of them to work their way into position. They barely made it in time. John Daisy pulled up in a tight ravine when he saw movement. He touched the Kid on the arm then silently pointed.

Disalin hadn't caught up and there were three. One was the scout Bonito, another was no more than a boy, but he carried a man's rifle. The third, neither John Daisy nor the Kid recognized, but he looked like an old wolf. They were on foot and coming fast.

"Let's do it," the Kid said, and they broke from cover, deliberately showing their backs. They scrambled over broken ground like they were in full flight. They were spotted immediately, and the three pursuers set up a whoop. The Kid and John Daisy were kicking up rocks and shale as they scrambled down each ravine and up the other side. They led the chase for ten minutes before they found the type of steep ravine they were looking for. They went over the top of the ridge and half slid, and half ran to the bottom. This was the spot.

John Daisy pulled up and the Kid kept going, up the other side. He was kicking up enough sign for two men. This side of the ravine was a slide with no cover and a long sloping rise to the top. Slipping and kicking, he worked his way up the hill, kicking over rocks as if in great haste. When he reached the top, he turned and looked back. John Daisy had vanished.

The Kid went over the rise. He went ten feet then turned and went parallel to the ridge for another twenty. He worked his way back up to the top, this time silently. There was a clump of ocotillo growing right on the edge and he snaked up to it. He lay flat and cautiously peered around it. Both pistols were ready, and he didn't expect a long wait.

He heard them before he saw them, as they scrambled up the

ridge across the way. They came over the top cautiously, but quickly. Seeing the ravine empty, they came sliding and skidding down to the bottom just like the Kid and John Daisy had done. The sign was as plain as day and they stayed right on it, coming up the other side.

When they were halfway up the slope, John Daisy suddenly appeared. He rose from behind them, where a clump of sage had been moments before. The Kid didn't see him until he moved. The dust and dirt fell off of him as he came up, but the Winchester was as shiny as ever.

The attackers had their backs to him, and their eyes were on the top of the ridge. The Kid was off to the side and as he stood up, he casually pointed both pistols at them.

"Howdy boys," he said in English at the same time John Daisy racked a shell into the Winchester. Of course, he didn't expect them to understand him, but they would know that the dance had started.

36

As soon as the Kid came up, John Daisy levered his yeller-belly and the pursuers knew they were in a hard spot. The scout, Bonito, and the older man froze. The boy stopped so suddenly that he fell sideways, sending rocks skittering back down the slope.

Bonito took a quick glance, over his shoulder, to the other slope. The old wolf did the same. Glancing at each other, they looked back at the Kid. Their faces were made of granite, their eyes cold and deep. They waited for the Kid to fire.

"Id adinat'ii" the yellow-haired Kid said, warning them not to move. They didn't, standing as if made of stone, looking up at this white man with pale eyes and long hair and knee-high buckskin moccasins.

Bonito's eyes glinted with recognition. He almost smiled. "Ugashe'."

The old man glanced at him, quizzically. "Ugashe'?" Bonito tipped his head slightly and nodded, "Shonto's ishki'in. Ochocama's ishki'in." His eyes didn't leave the Kid.

The older man looked back up at the Kid. He nodded his head, his eyes narrowing. "Ah," he said softly. "Shonto's ishki'in."

The Kid smiled down on them, "Pleased to make your acquaintance." He waggled a pistol at them. "Now, how about droppin' them shooters?"

They looked at him with uncomprehending eyes. He said it again in their language. They still just looked at him. The pistols were cocked, and they were running out of time, when Bonito slowly sat his carbine butt on the ground. He turned it loose, and it fell over, skidding down the rocks.

The other two began to do the same. There was a sudden movement from above, up and behind John Daisy. It was Disalin, and he'd moved a damn sight faster than the Kid ever expected. Disalin was as surprised as anyone else. He came over the top, his rifle in his left hand. John Daisy turned, bringing the Winchester around. Disalin went sideways, switching hands, his rifle exploding as he dived behind a dwarf pine.

Bonito and the older brave saw their chance and moved, one in each direction. The Kid fired both pistols across the ravine at Disalin, hoping to throw him off balance, and give John Daisy a chance for cover. The old wolf brought his rifle up and snapped a shot at the Kid. Being an uphill shot, it went high, snapping a small branch on the ocotillo. The Kid moved right, and going to one knee, fired at the old man as he moved. He missed and the old man was moving crab-like up the slope; he had the rifle barrel up and pointing at the Kid. The Kid thumbed the hammer and fired left-handed. The man's head snapped back like he had been poleaxed. His body dropped and skidded, his rifle firing into the rocks.

Across the way, Disalin and John Daisy had found cover and

were banging away at each other as fast as they could lever. The young boy had seen the old man shot and he was turned and trying to escape, skidding back down the slope.

The Kid turned away from the boy. Bonito dove around the ocotillo and slammed into him, his razor-sharp knife slashing at the Kid's midsection. Out of sheer reflex the Kid parried with his left hand, and there was a clang of metal as the knife bounced off the barrel of the pistol. The Kid felt the blade slice across the top of his wrist. The Kid went backwards, Bonito on top.

The Kid had a knee up and using the momentum, he kicked the scout up and over. The scout slid clear, and the Kid rolled hard. He came up and the man was on him again. The Kid had to drop the Walker to grab the scout's sleeve and pull him sideways. Bonito was half turned and slammed a hard elbow into the side of the Kid's cheek. The Kid ducked his head into the scout's shoulder and his free hand found the wrist of Bonito's knife hand. Bonito had his pistol trapped, holding his wrist tight against his body.

The two men strained, swinging around. The Kid's heel caught, and he felt himself going down. He snapped his gun hand down against the weak link in Bonito's grip, at the junction of the thumb and forefinger. As he fell, he pushed off. Between the snap of his wrist and the force of his fall, his gun hand came free. Using the momentum of the push, he kicked free and rolled as quick as he could several times. The hard, jagged chunks of rock gouged into his back. He came up about eight feet away. Bonito rolled swiftly up on his toes but unfortunately, he had brought a knife to what was now a gunfight.

The Apache scout was game and had as much heart as the

Kid had ever seen. His dark eyes were on the Kid as he screamed his challenge and charged with the knife. The Kid shot him in the throat. He went down and rolled over and was done.

The Kid instinctively took a step down the slope and turned, looking for the boy with the man-sized rifle. The boy had seen enough and was gone. Across the way John Daisy was firing up the hill at Disalin and Disalin was returning it. They both had found good cover and were just spending shells. The Kid fired across at Disalin, to give him something else to think about. Disalin snapped one in return, then turned and scrambled back over the hill. John Daisy started after him. The Kid pulled a bandana and began to wrap his bloody wrist.

He turned and looked at the body of Bonito for a long moment. "Can I borrow your horse?" he said.

37

John Daisy went up the slope at an angle, cresting the top at full speed, forty feet from where he figured Disalin would expect him. He came over low and fast, but Disalin wasn't waiting. He was several yards ahead, moving across the broken ground, threading between the mountain junipers and the boulders. John Daisy could only catch fleeting glimpses. He had no shot. Disalin was climbing. John Daisy was after him in an instant, a low growl in his throat.

Now it was a full-fledged foot race across the treacherous slope. In a few moments John Daisy could tell he was gaining. Disalin had spent much of his energy coming back across the canyon.

This sped John Daisy on, unmindful of the skin he was scraping off his palms and his knees as he scrambled through the rocks. Disalin was headed to a break at the top of the canyon. From this break, one man could hold off a hundred. But a glance over his shoulder told him that he wasn't going to make it. John Daisy was now only a few yards behind and gaining.

Disalin veered to the side and quickly climbed a short steep wall that led to a flat open grassy spot. It was several yards wide and a hundred feet long. Disalin pushed himself up over the top, his legs trembling with the effort. His chest was heaving in the thin air. John Daisy came up right behind him, almost as tired. As Disalin tried to bring his rifle up, John Daisy was on him. The two men went down hard in the rocky gramma grass. As they rolled, Disalin's rifle slipped from his hand and skittered across the flat. He grabbed at the Winchester in John Daisy's hands. As tired as he was, he was still a powerful man.

Disalin bent John Daisy's hand back and trapped the barrel of the rifle in the crook of his arm. He leaned forward, applying more pressure until John Daisy had to release the rifle. He clubbed Disalin in the side of the head. The rifle dropped into the tall grass as Disalin fell back from the force of the blow. He kept a grip on John Daisy and as he went backward, he flung John Daisy to the side.

Both men rolled up onto the balls of their feet and they both charged without hesitation. The sound of flesh and muscle striking flesh and muscle was large. John Daisy was disadvantaged because of his height. Disalin possessed a lower center of gravity, his muscles bunched and hard and knobby. Disalin had always been among the better wrestlers in the camp because of his short and powerful frame. John Daisy relied on his quickness and agility, but both men had been brought up in the rough and tumble ways of the rancheria.

The two men strained against each other, feet shuffling through the dusty grass, fighting for purchase. Disalin shoved up against the taller man and turning suddenly, he pinned John Daisy's arm under his own. His eyes were bright as he sensed victory. His hand searched for and found the soft flesh at the throat of the Coyotero. His powerful fingers began a relentless tightening, his thumb gouging into the hollow under John Daisy's ear.

John Daisy strained with all his strength against the shorter man, pushing the man back. Then with lightning speed, he lunged backwards, bringing Disalin with him. Using the man's weight against him, he flung him to the side, breaking Disalin's grip. John Daisy's breath was rasping from his bruised throat.

Both men, as one, reached to their knee-high leggings and pulled a long-bladed knife. They stood a pace apart, both gasping for breath, their eyes locked. They began to circle, the knives held slightly out and to the side, the cutting edge up.

John Daisy struck first, his hand a blur. His blade sliced the sleeve of Disalin's shirt but no blood came. Again they circled. Disalin knew what he had before him. He knew that when he killed this one, it would not be done. He would have to kill the white child, Ugashe', also. This would have to be done or he would spend the remainder of his life watching his back trail.

Disalin feinted a jab and John Daisy danced backwards. Disalin went in quickly, attacking with a wide slashing sweep. The tip of Disalin's knife sliced the front of John Daisy's shirt and a thin line of red appeared, staining the white, dust-covered cloth. John Daisy spun away, then reversing, he thrust upward to the soft belly of the man. Disalin skidded, stopping his own momentum, just in time to prevent becoming impaled. He jumped back and John Daisy came forward again, on the attack, slashing and cutting, driving the shorter man back.

John Daisy suddenly broke off the attack and the two men

circled again. This time John Daisy waited. He kept moving to his left and he waited. He knew that this one was arrogant and would not accept being driven backwards. This one would try to retrieve the initiative.

When Disalin lunged, John Daisy was ready. His hand snapped out and grasped Disalin's wrist. In one motion he swung the hand wide from the body then deliberately fell backwards, holding the man. He kicked his feet straight out, catching Disalin in both shins. Disalin's feet flew out from beneath him and John Daisy fell straight back, pulling the man on top. As they crashed backwards, John Daisy brought his knife up and in between their bodies. The tip sliced through the heavy chest muscle and slipped through the ribs. Disalin screamed as his life's blood flooded over John Daisy.

John Daisy lay for a brief moment, sucking air into his lungs before he struggled to shove the body off of him. He rolled to his feet looking at the dead man. He wiped the bloody knife against Disalin's shirt then with a sudden thought, he leaned down and stripped the spirit shirt from Disalin's body.

He straightened, holding the blood-soaked, buckskin shirt. He looked at the shirt, shaking his head.

"Lot of good this did you," he said to the dead man.

38

Cibicue Creek was a shallow, busy creek that whispered its song to the cottonwoods. These cottonwoods had been captivated for so many ages that their thick and sinewy branches now bowed forward, afraid to miss a note. The waters ran from the top of the world, through the canyon of the eagle's nest, where in a split second, the Cibicue waters merged, with a thundering rush, into the dark and murky waters of the Salt. Now as one they ran south to the desert below.

The Peoples of the Coyotero and Mimbrenos and Chircauhua, and even the Mescelaro had gathered here in this high rolling plain. They had come from all directions, men with their wives, families with children and single men. Even groups of women, two or three at a time. As they rode and walked into this special place they looked about and were amazed. They had not seen such a gathering. Even the old ones, who could remember the days before the coming of the whites, could not remember such a large gathering of *Is-his-Inday'*, the Men of the Woods.

The younger, more fiery warriors gathered around Gar,

accepting him as their leader, hoping in their breasts that this young scar-faced man was the one that would lead them to the times that their parents had told them about. Noch-ay-del-Klinne was the Spirit leader, the medicine that bound them, but Gar would be the spear that the Dreamer would use to slay their enemies.

Upon Noch-ay-del-Klinne's arrival the dances had started immediately. Even as the camp was being set up, many of the followers did not wait. There was a sense of urgency that was present, a feverish feeling that this was the gathering that would determine their future. There had never been a gathering more important than this.

While Noch-ay-del-Klinne meditated, and, at times, joined his dancers, Gar took charge of the camp, determining what groups would camp where, putting the strongest and most radical together. He ordered bands of hunters to forage for food. Nalin oversaw the preparation of the great meals by the women, settling the small disputes that inevitably arose. It was a mark of great respect that the women allowed this leadership from such a young woman. Noch-ay-del-Klinne watched his daughter and was proud at how she was holding this gathering together.

The hunters were lucky and found a great herd of antelope, numbering in the hundreds. A good many were slaughtered, and this was a good sign. Noch-ay-del-Klinne immediately proclaimed this an omen, an omen the spirits had sent to approve of the gathering.

While there had been dancing all day, the main dancing began at dark, and at dusk of the first day, the dancers were already in a frenzy and many claimed visions. When Noch-ay-del-Klinne and his daughter joined in, the cry from the hundreds of throats was thunderous and deafening. These two were now the royalty of all the tribes and all the clans had found some way to connect the Dreamer and his daughter to their blood lines.

These people had spent their lives traveling in small family units or rancherias that supported only a handful of families. To look about them, at this gathering beside the waters of the Cibicue, was a thing of amazement. Never had there been such numbers of Dinee together.

The tall, lean, young man the whites called the Kid brought Bonito's pony to the edge of the crest of the slope. He stopped just shy, not wanting to outline himself against the lighter sky. John Daisy reined the big spotted mare up beside him. Although the camp was a good two miles away, they could hear the chanting and smell the dust in the summer air.

The day had been a hot one, with the sun bright and blazing, but now the sun was under the western horizon and the air was beginning to cool. The two young grandsons of Ochocama leaned against a boulder, studying the distant twinkling of campfires. John Daisy had been amazed at the numbers. What he saw before him was staggering. The lights stretched back away from the ribbon of water as far as the eye could see. The Kid swore softly at the sight.

The sky was rosy red where the sun had disappeared. The Kid spoke, his voice low in the night, "I remember Shonto telling of seeing a gathering of the plains tribes, the Lakota and Cheyenne and Arapahoe that was like this. He said their teepee's stretched for miles, over the horizon." He shook his head. "I never would have believed that the tribes would ever agree on one single thing, let alone to come together like this."

The Kid pushed his hat back so that it hung by the leather throng down his back. He ran his fingers through his long blond hair, then deftly tied it back with a blue bandana. In the dusk, he looked Apache, like the man next to him. He turned slightly in the saddle and studied John Daisy. Even in the cooling dark, he could sense the trouble in his shik'isn's heart. He looked back down the slope, then urged his pony on over the crest.

"This could turn into a real shit-show," he said

"Already is, " John Daisy returned, moving the appaloosa up with him.

They walked their ponies silently down the long slope toward the distant lights. They took their time, letting the last of the light fade. They reached the outer limits of the camp unchallenged. There were no guards, just an occasional dog. They could see a great flat area just up from the creek bank. It was there that a huge fire blazed, surrounded by an undulating mass of people flitting from the light to the dark. Everyone was at the fire. The Kid and John Daisy mounted their ponies, then walked them openly into the camp.

This is where Noch-ay-del-Klinne was and this is where they would speak with him. The outer ring of people were the old women and children, then the younger women, some of whom were dancing, then the young men. John Daisy gently moved the big mare into these, and they glanced at him and gave way, allowing him and the Kid in.

Atop their mounts the two could see over the heads of those in front. They brought their mounts to within a dozen yards of the dancers and were finally stopped by the wall of bodies pressed together.

In the dim and flickering firelight, they saw the prophet seated in front of the large wickiup that was, no doubt, his and Nalin's. His head was back, his eyes closed in meditation. His forearms rested on each knee, palms up. The chanting was deafening, but he sat as if oblivious to his surroundings. To his right side, sat Nalin, her head bowed and shoulders hunched, as if exhausted. Tendrils of hair had escaped her normally fastidious hair combs and damply bracketed her face. Gar was in among the dancers, his drenched and glistening body naked, save for a breechcloth. His head was back, his face tight with ecstasy, his dancing more fervent than the others. The scar on his cheek picked up the color of the fire and shined in the darkness.

The fire played stark and eerie tricks across the faces of the dancers. These dancers bounced in and out of the shadows like blinking rapidly on a bright day. John Daisy could feel the rhythm of the chanting rising in his blood. He glanced across at Ugashe' and could see by the brightness in the white child's eyes that he felt the same.

Across the fire, Nalin stirred, slowly raising her head. She looked drawn and tired, but she sat straighter, her mouth moving with the chanting. Her hair was held back by the combs. Bits of bright colored cloth were tied to the ends. She was dressed in the same white buckskin dress with the ornate beading she had worn for the dancing at Ochocama's.

As the two mounted men watched riveted, the girl struggled to her feet. She swayed with exhaustion. A roar came from the circle of chanters as she was urged to rejoin the dancers. The chanting throng now caught up her name, trying to build her strength, and her will, by the force of their voices. The girl took a deep breath then shuddered, her skin rippling like a horse shaking off a bottle fly. She turned to join the dance.

She opened her eyes, and they were deceptively bright, not showing the exhaustion her body felt. She stepped into the circle of dancers, moving forward. At three unsteady steps, she suddenly stopped. Her eyes bore through the flickering darkness and came to light on the man astride the spotted horse. Her face was drained and pale as her eyes flicked from John Daisy to the Kid and back. She stood stock still, as if riveted to the spot. Slowly the mass of people turned to see what had caught her attention and as they did this, the sound of the chanting diminished until all were turned. The chanting was gone like the smoke in the breeze.

In the sudden silence the girl took a faltering step forward. "Chan-Deisi," she said, then she lost her remaining strength and crumpled to the ground.

39

John Daisy slid off the appaloosa to rush to Nalin's side, but Gar reached her first. Gripping her arms, he helped the struggling girl to her feet. Gar's face was twisted with anger, but there was something else. There was surprise. "Why do you come here?" he asked harshly.

John Daisy ignored Gar; his concern was for the girl. Without thinking, he reached a hand out to her. Her eyes were on him, and she took his hand, stepping from Gar's grasp. This gesture was not missed by those watching, and Gar's face went from angry to livid. It seemed for a brief moment that Gar would attack John Daisy.

Then a voice rang out. "It is good." The people turned to look at Noch-ay-del-Klinne, his voice loud in the night. "It is good that my friend Ochocama's grandson joins us!" The medicine man was on his feet and had walked into the center of dancers. The people jostled to give him room.

He reached Nalin and taking her arm from John Daisy, he turned to the women closest. "Help my daughter to my lodge. She must lie down to rest."

"But, father," Nalin began to protest.

He held up a restraining hand, "Go now," he said quietly.

Two of the women came up and helped her away. The old man turned back to John Daisy, looking past him at the Kid. "And, also here, we have with us the one we call Ugashe'." He gestured, "Come, step down and join us."

The Kid slid off his mount and stepped into the firelight. His eyes found Gar's and the hatred in Gar's eyes was stark and deep. The Kid held Gar's gaze for a long moment before turning to the small man. The Kid was startled at how old the medicine man looked.

"It is good to see my grandfather's oldest friend again," the Kid said evenly. "We have ridden a long way to find you; it is important that we talk."

Noch-ay-del-Klinne swept his hand across and away from his chest in an expansive manner, "Speak to me, Ugashe'. You are among friends here." He turned and looked at the mass of attentive faces in a dramatic fashion. "You grew up with many of these people in your rancheria."

"He has forgotten!" Gar spit. "He has not seen them since they were forced onto the reservation." He stepped forward, glaring, "This white man roams freely, he is not forced onto the hair-face prison."

"I roam freely," John Daisy said. "And I am not white."

"Yes, my son, you do," Noch-ay-del-Klinne said. "But you are one man, you are not a people." The prophet's voice was soothing now. "Do you come this night to tell me that you have decided, Chan-Deisi?" He looked deep into the young man. "Have you decided?"

John Daisy sadly shook his head, "It has already been decided." He turned and looked at the Kid.

"The blue-coats come," the Kid said. "Two full troops of the blue-coated soldiers come now to take you back to the agency." A murmur ran through the crowd. "Either take you back," the Kid repeated. "Or kill you!" There was a groan of protest from a hundred throats, but the medicine man was not perturbed

The Kid continued, "Their nantan is a man called Tibbet. I am told that he is very ambitious. I am told that he will stop at nothing to become an even bigger nantan in the hair-face army. This man is dangerous. This man is cunning. He knows that if he brings you back, the chiefs in Washington will be pleased. If you and your young warriors resist and he brings you back dead, he would have much medicine. The white people still remember the killing of Nantan yella hair Custer."

Noch-ay-del-Klinne turned and looked at John Daisy, "Is this so?"

"If Ugashe' says it, then it is so," John Daisy said quietly.

Gar could stay still no longer; he swung around to address his followers, "I say, if the hair-face comes, we meet him here." His warriors roared agreement as he swung back to Noch-ay-del-Klinne. "I say we meet this Tibbet here at Cibicue! Meet him with lance and bow and gun. Meet him with the ones that went before and meet him wearing the magic of the spirit shirts!" Hundreds of the surrounding men roared their agreement raising their fists to the air.

John Daisy stepped to the appaloosa and pulled something from his roll. He turned back to Gar. Moving quickly to where Gar stood, he wadded Disalin's spirit shirt and threw it at Gar's feet. Gar was surprised but did not move. One of the closer braves picked it up, and as the crowd recognized it, they grew quieter.

"This spirit shirt," John Daisy said in a loud, contemptuous voice, "did not stop Disalin from joining his ancestors!"

Gar would have jumped at John Daisy, but Noch-ay-del-Klinne stepped in between. He held up a hand. "Quiet!" he called, then again, loudly, "Quiet!"

Slowly the crowd grew silent. Nalin had come back out of the wickiup and now appeared again, beside her father. She took his arm, "Come, father," she said just loud enough. "You must think on this, you must decide what is best for our people."

Her father looked up into his daughter's face and after a moment he nodded. "Yes," he agreed. "This is not an easy thing." He turned and his eyes looked to the southeast, the direction from which the white troops would come. He was silent a long moment then turned and spoke to no one in particular. "Find food for my guests Chan-Deisi and Ugashe'." He reached a hand out and took Nalin's hand in his. "Come child, I will need your strength."

40

Just as Sergeant Barnes feared, half the troop's horses were bloated and sick and almost impossible to control. Halfway through the day's march the colonel's own mount made a gaseous, wet green mess while the colonel was standing near, and his polished boots were splattered with the vile smelling stuff. The little colonel lost his temper and ordered Dandy Jim stripped of his weapons and placed under arrest.

Lieutenant Gatewood had guessed correctly, and it was fading light before they bivouacked beside Carrizo Creek. Under Gatewood's suggestion, the horses were placed under the care of a squad of the white troopers. Gatewood ordered the Apache scouts to camp in closer than normal. He wanted to keep an eye on them.

It was after the inky blackness had taken over, but before the moon was up, that one of the scouts approached Gatewood at his small fire. It was a man they called Mose. He was the sergeant of the scouts, and now, after what had been transpiring, one of the few left that Gatewood still trusted. The man was short and slender, but very wiry. Gatewood knew him to be a tough man in a fight and had served with him for several years.

The lieutenant had been working on his journal, but he now set it aside at the other man's approach. Mose stepped into the firelight, his dark, coppery skin glistening.

"Sergeant Mose," Gatewood proclaimed, by way of greeting.

Mose smiled nervously, his teeth catching the light. "Mose come to

Nantan Long Nose, need to talk."

The Lieutenant waved to a spot in the grass beside him and Mose settled down, cross-legged. "Speak what's on your mind, sergeant."

Mose glanced around to ensure no one was in earshot. Lowering his voice he said, "Mose has spoke with many scouts. Many here, many at the agency. Many of these have been to see Noch-ay-del-Klinne. Many have danced." He paused, leaning forward, "All say there will be much trouble. Many will die."

Gatewood waved a hand, irritated. "That will depend on Noch-ay-del-Klinne."

Mose nodded his head, "It is so. The prophet will decide. But Nantan Tibbet will not allow Noch-ay-del-Klinne to decide any other way. Tibbet will make it only one way." He shrugged a small shrug. "Then many will die."

Lieutenant Gatewood sat silently a moment, then reached for his cherrywood pipe and began to pack it. He did this very deliberately. Finally, he said, "I am a soldier, Mose, just as you. We only follow orders. Noch-ay-del-Klinne must return to the agency. If he does not, we will take him back."

Mose nodded, "Noch-ay-del-Klinne will go back. He will go back if the nantan allows it."

Gatewood looked hard at the other man, finally he said, "This is so?"

Mose nodded.

Gatewood lit the pipe, taking long draws. Once it was going well, he asked, "What is it you wish of me?"

"I wish Nantan Long Nose to ask the Nantan Tibbet to allow me to ride ahead and talk with Noch-ay-del-Klinne. If I talk with him first, he can decide to return."

"You think you can convince him to return peacefully?"

Again Mose shrugged, "If I talk with him then he knows. Then it is up to Noch-ay-del-Klinne who will live and who will die and not the little nantan."

Gatewood stared out past the fire, into the darkness. He sat like this for a long time. Mose sat silently waiting, his eyes never leaving the lieutenant's face.

Finally, Gatewood said, "Let's go talk to Major Redding."

The moon was high when the young, fresh-faced major was buttoning his tunic as he made his way across the camp, toward the lighted tent of Colonel Tibbet. He slowed just enough to allow himself time to finish the final button, then he stepped to the front of the tent and lightly tapped on the center support.

"Come!"

He pulled the flap back and stepped into the full-sized tent. The colonel was sitting on the side of his bunk, making an entry into his report. He glanced up. "What is it major, more sick horses?"

"No sir," Major Redding replied evenly, trying to not let his dislike for the man show. "Lieutenant Gatewood has suggested that we send a man ahead."

The colonel's head came up, the yellow light from the kerosene lantern making his eyes dark and his skin a pasty yellow. "For what purpose, lieutenant?"

Major Redding stepped further into the tent, allowing the flap to fall free behind him. "He thinks that if this medicine man, Nochay-del-Klinne is given the opportunity to surrender, he will do so. Gatewood's afraid that some of the man's young bucks will shoot first and we'll end up with a full-scale bloodletting."

The colonel stared at him in the flickering light. His face was expressionless. Finally he spoke. "Gatewood wants to warn the man, so he can escape?"

"No sir," Redding said. "The man could escape on his own, anytime, Gatewood says."

"Lieutenant Gatewood, major!" Tibbet said.

"Yessir, Lieutenant Gatewood, sir. He says that he doesn't figure the man to run because he has no place to run to. The scouts would eventually find him anyway, sir. No matter where he was." The young major swallowed. "I agree with him, sir."

The little colonel slowly nodded his head, his eyes boring into the young man. "You agree."

Major Redding nodded, knowing he was on dangerous political ground. "Yessir, I believe we should take every opportunity to avoid unnecessary bloodshed."

"And, if I don't agree, major?"

"If there is bloodshed, you wouldn't look very good at an inquiry, sir."

"I wouldn't?"

Major Redding looked the man in the eye, "No sir, you wouldn't. Not in the light of my report, sir."

"Your report, major?" The little man stood now, but not angry. He appeared to be almost amused. "Your written report?"

"Yessir, my written report."

"And what would your report say?"

"That you ignored your senior officer's advice on permitting the insurrectionist to surrender, sir."

Colonel Tibbet studied the taller, younger man for several long, silent moments. Finally, he said, "I trust you like this post assignment, major." Before Redding could answer, he continued, "Because you're going to be assigned here for a very long time."

The young major held the colonel's look. "I've always figured that I would be here much longer than you, sir," he said, evenly.

Again, Colonel Tibbet seemed amused. "It's my understanding that your pretty young wife doesn't like it out here. She'll probably stay back east with her folks." He turned and sat again on the cot. "Send your man, major," he said, turning his attention back to his logbook. "It won't make a bit of difference."

"Yessir," Redding said, moving through the flap and out into the darkness where Gatewood and Mose were waiting.

41

It was deep into the night and the inside of the large wickiup was filled with the pungent odor of the smoke from the medicine man's pipe. Noch-ay-del-Klinne sat cross- legged beside the tiniest of fires, feeding it occasionally with small twigs and pinches of his tobacco. His black eyes were troubled as he stared into the flames, seeking solutions.

Nalin had managed to doze. When she awakened, she felt as if only two or three hours had passed. Suddenly, she was awake, and she knew she would sleep no more this night. She sat up and quietly studied her father. For a very long time they sat like this, Noch-ay-del-Klinne studying the flames and Nalin studying him. Finally, Noch-ay-del-Klinne turned his head and looked at the girl. She saw that his face was haggard, his eyes sad and troubled.

Nalin had sat with her own thoughts, and in a woman's way, the path was clear to her. She didn't understand why her father didn't understand it as well as she did. "They will kill you," she said simply.

He shrugged. "If they do," he spoke quietly, "it will not

matter. He studied his medicine pipe for a moment. "I will admit," he continued, "that I believe as Chan-Deisi. The spirit shirts have lost their magic." He said this with a hint of a smile.

"Father," she said softly, "I never did believe they could stop a blue-coat bullet. And Chan-Deisi is right on other matters also. There are too many indaa. They are like grains of dust. When one blows away, there are always more. And they have too many nantans. They do not speak the same. One will give his word, then he is gone, and another comes and changes the words."

"I have led the dances," her father said, his words so low that Nalin had to lean forward to catch them. "I have seen the vision. I have talked with the *ones that came before*. Am I to forsake it now?"

Nalin slowly shook her head, her eyes filling with emotion. "My father. I am your first follower. I have experienced the power of the dance. I have felt the spirits and I have seen visions of the land the way it was before the whites came." Her voice caught and she struggled to continue. "But Chan-Deisi is right. There are too many."

Her father was suddenly angry. "Are we to suffer at the hands of these whites? Accepting their meager rations and threadbare blankets. Are we to raise our children to sit in their lodges and drink tizwin and wait for the next feeding, like a dog? Are we to live as cattle?"

The tears were now rolling down the soft, luminous cheeks of the girl. "That is one choice," she said, her voice soft in the darkness. "The other is to die."

Noch-ay-del-Klinne reached across and touched his daughter, his face reflecting the tenderness and love he had for her. "What counsel would my daughter give me?"

She leaned forward, taking her father's hand, her face upturned. "Let the People scatter like the dust in the wind. Let us leave now and go with Ochocama to the Madres. We can hide there, until there is a better time."

"Will there ever be a better time?"

"Anything is better than waiting here to be killed by the small-chin nantan!"

Noch-ay-del-Klinne slowly leaned back, freeing himself from her hand. He reached up and smoothed the coal-black hair away from her face. "What will Gar say?" he asked softly.

"You know what Gar will say. He will tell the people to believe in the shirts. To believe that the *ones who came before* will save us."

"And now you say that Noch-ay-del-Klinne should go out and tell his people that suddenly, in the face of these soldiers, he does not believe?"

Nalin looked into her father's face and for the first time this night, saw the resolve in the lines of his face. And she knew that it had been there all along. Even from the first day. Her head bowed and her eyes closed, and she felt the despair wash over her heart.

42

In the deepest part of the night, the camp was at rest. No one had gone back to their lodges but had brought their blankets to the great fire and lay facing toward the entrance to Noch-ay-del-Klinne's lodge. Like a giant pin wheel, they lay around the mound of embers of the dancing fire.

The Kid and John Daisy lay beside their ground picketed horses, rolled in their blankets. Sleeping, but aware of every movement, every unusual sound. Two hours before the first light of dawn a commotion started on the outskirts of the camp. It began with the barking of several dogs and then the murmur of distant voices. There were visitors riding in.

John Daisy rolled up to his feet and the Kid sat up, untangling his legs from the blanket. His hand held the pistol that he usually slept with. With a small movement, he slid it into the holster that lay beside him.

Across the camp, two men walked their ponies toward the glowing light of the great pile of red embers. At first, they were only silhouettes in the darkness, and as they drew closer the Kid could see the shiny buttons of a blue-coat soldier's field jacket.

"One is called Mose. Don't know the other," John Daisy said quietly, lowering the barrel of the Winchester.

The flap to the entrance to Noch-ay-del-Klinne's wickiup slid back and the diminutive prophet stepped out. He stood still, watching the two men ride up. They pulled their ponies up to the glow of the dying fire and dismounted.

"Ain't here to dance," the Kid said. John Daisy grunted. The one John Daisy had called Mose stepped forward. He held his hand straight out in greeting. "Noch-ay-del-Klinne."

"I am Noch-ay-del-Klinne," said the small man.

"I am Gian-nah-tah, of the Eagle clan. I am called Mose by the indaa."

The small medicine man nodded. "I know of Gian-nah-tah. Why does he come to my fire at this hour before the dawn?"

"Not real friendly," the Kid muttered. John Daisy ignored him, wishing him to be quiet.

Mose's expression didn't change. "I am sent by Nantan Large Nose. He wants you to know that you must return with him to San Carlos. If you do not, he wants you to know that his nantan, the little one, will take you. It does not matter to him if he kills you and many others, to do so. There are many soldiers and many guns."

As Mose was speaking, Nalin had stepped out beside her father. The old man turned to look at his daughter. "You see," he said. "It is already decided."

"It is never too late," she said.

Noch-ay-del-Klinne turned back, but not to Mose. This time he faced the Kid. "Ugashe'" he spoke. "Will you go with Gian-nah-tah and tell this little nantan that I will come in three days.

Tell him that I need rest from the dancing, and I need time to pack for the journey."

The Kid slung his pistol belt around his narrow hips. "I will go old one, but the Nantan Tibbet will not listen." His eyes saw the fear in Nalin's face. "He is moving already."

Noch-ay-del-Klinne shrugged, turning back inside the lodge. "Tomorrow will be tomorrow," he said in a voice so soft it was barely audible.

43

When the light in the sky was up enough to see by, Colonel Tibbet rose from his cot and began his morning rituals. Pouring water into his tin cup, he unscrewed the top to the silver metal case holding his toothbrush. Wetting the brush, he dipped it into the white tooth powder and vigorously began to scrub his teeth. Two hundred down strokes, two hundred side strokes. Rinse the brush, then one hundred strokes with clean water.

He washed his hands and face several times then finally donned his uniform. Not his khaki traveling uniform, but the one with the ribbons and medals he had kept wrapped just for today. By the time he was ready for mess he was dressed as if ready for the parade ground. Wrapping the belt to his sword around his middle he heard a commotion coming from the north end of the camp. He pulled back the flap of his tent and barked, "What's goin' on out there, soldier?"

The sentry snapped to attention, "Sounds like one of the men on watch, sir. Sounds like someone's comin' in."

Major Redding and Lieutenant Gatewood had been out of their bedrolls since before light. They shared a small pot of coffee and were sitting, gnawing on hard biscuit and fatback. When the sentry sounded the alarm, they sprang to their feet.

"Must be Mose," Gatewood guessed, striding rapidly toward where the sound was emanating. Major Redding was right on his heels.

When they reached the guard, they found him rifle up, in a casual stance. He glanced around at their approach. As they stepped up beside him, he said, "Three of them comin' in, sir. Right down the canyon there." With the barrel of his rifle, he indicated a break where the creek turned a corner. Sure enough, three horsemen came into sight and rode toward them, single file. They were a hundred-fifty yards away. They rode with no urgency. Even from that distance both Gatewood and the major recognized the lead rider as Sergeant Mose. The second man was a mystery, wearing a flat-brimmed hat, the beginning sun making it look as if his hair was light yellow as it hung down his back.

Major Redding's face suddenly relaxed; he swore softly. Gatewood glanced at him, puzzled. "Who is it?"

"It's the Kid." He shook his head. "That boy turns up in the damndest places!"

It was moments, then the three riders were abreast of the waiting officers. The Kid swung Bonito's pony around, then up in front and pulled it to a halt.

"You show up in the damndest places, Kid," the major said. "But I don't recognize the horse."

"I lost yours, so I brought you another," the Kid said. "We need to see the colonel. It's important."

A short time later Colonel Tibbet stared at the Kid with an incredulous look, then threw his head back in a short and caustic laugh. He was the only one amused.

The amusement left in a hurry. "Three days!" he growled. He thrust a gloved finger at Lieutenant Gatewood. "Hell man, that's what that injun told you before, then he turned and ran!" He glared at the Kid. "What do you take me for, a fool?"

The Kid's eyes were even and cold. "Mister, I'm not here to take you for a drink of water. I'm just here to deliver the message."

"You will address me as colonel," Tibbet said coldly.

The big civilian scout, Booker, had joined them, coming up from where the command was bivouacked. He was looking at the Kid. "You tellin' us that you've been in that camp?"

The Kid turned his head to look at him, but he didn't answer.

"You just come and go as you please?" the scout pressed, making his point.

The colonel said, "That is odd." His eyes narrowed as he switched his gaze from Booker to the Kid. "Just how is it that you can do that?"

Major Redding spoke. "Sir, the Kid here was raised with'm. He was raised by Ochocama. He knows half the people in that camp."

Booker spit a stream of tobacco juice, then wiped his mouth on his sleeve. "When the shit hits the wind, Kid, whose side will you be on?"

The Kid's gaze was still cool and level. He didn't answer.

The colonel looked hard at the Kid. "You better get your head right," he said coldly. "You walk the wrong side and I'll throw you in the brig for a long time." He turned to Redding. "We are wasting time here. Major, have the men mounted and ready in twenty minutes. We are going into that camp and arrest the trouble-maker."

Twenty minutes later the colonel's order was made good, and the packers had the mule train packed and the troopers were mounted. Colonel Tibbet gave the signal and the column started moving. Up ahead, Major Redding and Lieutenant Gatewood moved at a faster pace with Mose and a dozen Apache scouts. They intended to get a mile out front. The scouts rode on either side of the trail, spreading out.

The Kid kicked his horse and galloped past the line of calvary, until he was beside Major Redding. "I'd like to give you a piece of advice," he said in a voice low enough to only be heard by the two of them. Major Redding looked across and nodded.

"I'd have those scouts ridin' single file," the Kid said. "When we get closer some of them will skip and join Gar's group. Single file will make it easier to know which scout is yours and which is Gars."

The major nodded, then signaled Gatewood up beside them and gave the order. The two young men rode in silence, side by side for a good distance. Later, as they began the climb out of the canyon, Redding glanced over and asked, "Where's your Indian friend. Has he joined them?"

The Kid shook his head, "Not yet. He's sweet on Noch-ay-del-Klinne's daughter and loyal to his grandfather so he's trying to protect both of them from what is inevitable. He will try to keep Gar from starting a war."

The major urged his mount up over a ridge of boulders. "Let's hope he's successful," he said.

It was early afternoon when they broke through the higher

ridges and emerged onto the flats. For the last hour they had begun to spot sentinels openly watching them, some on horseback, some on foot. All were bare to the waist, and many were painted. But they made no hostile move. As the column moved closer to the encampment, several braves on horseback became more daring and rode out to within a hundred yards of the column.

Many were whooping and shaking their rifles and hurling insults. Some of the more aggressive ones galloped up and down the column, shrilly whooping and taunting the cavalrymen. Gatewood rode calmly up and down, talking to his scouts and to the troopers, soothing jittery nerves. As the Kid predicted, several of the scouts had suddenly disappeared.

Major Redding and the Kid had dropped to the back of the scouts, and the column headed by Colonel Tibbet and the civilian scout, Booker, had closed to within three hundred yards. Suddenly from over a rise came a single horseman. His face was painted, upper half black and lower half white. He wore a pale, white buckskin shirt and carried a carbine. Whooping at the top of his lungs, he galloped at full speed to within just a few feet of Major Redding. He wheeled his mount, bringing it to a skidding halt. The young major's mount shied, and he fought it under control. It was Gar, and his face was twisted with contempt.

He shouted something in Dinee in a loud voice.

Redding glanced at the Kid and the Kid interpreted, "He wants to know what you can do here?" The Kid smiled, "He calls you a raw virgin chief."

Redding grinned. He reined his mount around to directly face the Indian. His eyes riveted to Gar, he reached down and unbuttoned the flap to his pistol holster. "Get out of the way of this column and stay away from it or I will shoot you myself."

Gar's eyes were black with fury and a cold sneer curled his lip. He turned to the Kid. "You have chosen to be white now, eh, Ugashe'?"

"Never had to choose," the Kid said, his eyes never leaving Gar's. His hand rested lightly on the horn of his saddle, just a heartbeat away from the butt of his belly gun.

Gar leaned over and spit on the ground. He pulled the pony around so hard that the animal squealed. He kicked the horse and it reared, then thundered away.

Mose rode up at this moment, his dark eyes watching Gar ride away. He muttered, "*Dan Juda*! All bad!"

By midafternoon, they came over the last rise and the camp stretched out before them. Major Redding sat with narrowed eyes studying the sight before him. "Jesus Christ!" he whistled. " There must be five hundred of them camped here."

He glanced back over his shoulder to where Tibbet and troops C and D were drawing up. "Seems like the colonel may be a little under manned."

"Has been all along," the Kid said.

They sat quietly, waiting for the column to catch up. The major was thinking the fort and reinforcements were one helluva long way away.

44

Noch-ay-del-Klinne stood in the dusty doorway of his lodge, watching the long, thin double line of blue-coat soldiers wind its way down the long grassy slope and into the camp. Colonel Tibbet led the column flanked by the baby-faced major and Lieutenant Gatewood. Behind them rode Booker and a company of calvary. Then came the pack train and the second company bringing up the rear.

The Apache scouts had come in slightly ahead of Tibbet and the Kid had come in with them. They dispersed into the waiting throng and intermingled, greeting friends and family. The Kid had walked his pony over to stand beside John Daisy, who had been waiting astride the appaloosa. The only scout that had stayed with the column was Mose and he rode beside Gatewood.

Gar was astride his brown and white pinto and now he brought it around toward the oncoming troops. He rode up to the front of the column and began riding his pony back and forth in front of Tibbet. It was his silent challenge. As the column moved through the camp, there was dead silence, with only the creak of leather and the occasional blowing of a horse.

Gar continued his silent taunting and Tibbet pressed on, ignoring the painted man. The little colonel was ramrod stiff in the saddle, his boots and hat brim gleaming, his uniform immaculate. The Kid watched the man, and while he didn't like Tibbet for a penny, he had to admire the soldier's gumption.

The column came straight into the heart of the camp and the people parted, allowing them a path. The intermingled tribes lined both sides of the path, four to five deep. Most of the troopers had sweated through their collars. Tibbet kept them moving forward, toward the ashes of the dancing fire. Tibbet could see the larger than normal wickiup and he saw the small but almost regal man standing there, waiting. A pace away from the man was a tall, beautiful young Indian woman.

Twenty-five paces from the medicine man he lifted a gloved hand and brought the column to a halt. As the column came to a disciplined stop, the crowd pressed in and the mounts began to fidget nervously. Tibbet sat silently, enjoying his dramatic moment.

Under his breath, to Gatewood, Major Redding said, "He thinks he's Caesar entering Rome."

It was obvious that the little colonel was enjoying himself immensely. Colonel Tibbet hiked around in his McClellan saddle and motioned to Major Redding. Major Redding, in turn, motioned up Mose, and they both came up beside the colonel.

As they drew abreast, Tibbet asked, casually, "Which is the insurrectionist? The one called Noch-ay-del-Klinne?"

Mose turned and, with a slight hesitation, pointed out the diminutive figure of the prophet. Noch-ay-del-Klinne's face was impassive and calm. Gar had dismounted and had moved up to defiantly face the soldiers.

Colonel Tibbet studied the medicine man, obviously interested in what his adversary was like. Finally, he said, "Tell him that these people must disperse and return to the reservation immediately. Tell him that I am here to take him into custody and return him to the agency."

Mose translated this, and then it was Noch-ay-del-Klinne's turn to study the nantan of the hair-face soldiers. He looked almost amused at Mose's translation. After a brief pause, the medicine man spoke. It was a short sentence. Tibbet looked to Mose.

"He says that his people are at home," Mose explained.

This irritated Tibbet. "Tell him this!" he said sternly. "The treaties signed many years ago say that home for these people is at San Carlos. These people must disperse and go there, now. The dances must stop for a little while. Tell him that no harm will come to him or any of his people unless he resists my command."

Noch-ay-del-Klinne listened to this intently, as did the rest of the people gathered round. Digesting this, Noch-ay-del-Klinne frowned. "Say to this nantan that I cannot go now," he said to Mose. "I have many matters of importance to attend to before leaving this place. Say that if the soldiers will return to their post, I will follow soon within three or four days."

Mose translated this and Colonel Tibbet immediately shook his head, "No, that will not do! Tell him that he comes with me now!"

As Mose translated this, a shock ran through the crowd and an angry murmur sprang up. The Kid's hand subconsciously touched the handle of his pistol. He leaned toward John Daisy and in a very low voice, asked, "When the shootin' starts, which side are we on?"

Without turning his head, John Daisy shrugged his shoulders. He kneed the appaloosa and walked it to where Nalin stood beside her father.

"Noch-ay-del-Klinne," John Daisy said in the Dinee tongue. "This hair-face nantan is foolish, but he is also very dangerous. We have many people and surely many of the hair- faces would die if you resist. But they have rifles that shoot many times before reloading. They have pistols that shoot many times. Look about you and see the faces of the women and the children. Many would die. You would certainly die as would this little nantan."

He raised his hand, palm out. "It is not our way, to spend life foolishly. Is it not better to live today? Leave the fight and the dance with the spirits for another day?" He pointed to Nalin, then to some of the other women gathered by her. "Ask your daughter. Ask the women. Ask them, if while they would sing the death song for their lost husbands and fathers, that they would not also scorn them for foolishly throwing their life away? Is it not the dinee way to live today unless there is no other choice? Do we not have a choice today?"

The crowd was silenced by John Daisy's words. Nalin stepped forward. "It is so," she said for all to hear. "Chan-Deisi speaks true."

Gar stepped up, his voice strong with anger. "Chan-Deisi speaks as a woman." He carried his carbine in his hand as if ready to use it. He beseeched Noch-ay-del-Klinne, "Look about you father, your warriors are ready to fight. Can you not see them? Yes, the hair-faces have guns that shoot many times, but we are many and we have our spirit shirts and we have the 'ones that have gone before'. We are five to their one, we cannot lose!"

John Daisy spoke evenly, "Yes, we can kill the hair-faces here, then they will send five times as many again, then when we kill them they will send ten times as many!"

Noch-ay-del-Klinne stood as if made of stone. Mose turned his head slightly and muttered something urgently over his shoulder to Lieutenant Gatewood. Instantaneously, Gatewood's voice rang through the camp. "Lock and load!"

The squad sergeants repeated the cry. "Lock and load!"

Many of the soldiers were frightened, but they were well trained, and as one their rifles cleared the leather cases, and the first cartridge was rammed home. Suddenly, Nalin dropped to her knees. Lifting her hands to the cloudless sky she began the high keening wail of the death song mourning the loss of her father. After a brief, stunned moment, another woman dropped to her knees and took up the song. Then another and yet another, until many of the woman were crying the loss of their loved ones.

Even the veteran troopers had never seen anything like this, and the hair rose at the nape of their necks. The warriors were shocked and stood mute. Noch-ay-del-Klinne finally moved, turning to the young man, Gar.

Noch-ay-del-Klinne's eyes were sad and defeated. He said, "I will go."

Gar's expression was twisted with contempt. Noch-ay-del-Klinne turned away and gently took Nalin's outstretched hand and lifted her to her feet. The wailing died away.

The small prophet looked up at John Daisy. "Tell the nantan that I will go with him."

Colonel Tibbet listened to the translation impassively then, without turning his head, "Major Redding, ask Mr. Booker up."

Redding turned and called, "Mr. Booker, to the column front, sir!"

Booker brought his horse up abreast of the colonel's and Colonel Tibbet said, "Mr. Booker, you and Sergeant Mose are to take command of the prisoner. You will permit no harm to come to his person. But," he paused here for emphasis, "if he attempts to escape, or if any of his people try to interfere, shoot him dead!"

The big scout leaned off the side of his mount and spit a brown stream to the ground. "Happy to, colonel."

Tibbett raised his hand and with his gloved forefinger he drew a horizontal circle in the air. He then pulled his mount around and as the troopers moved aside he rode back, down the middle of his command, followed by troopers as they wheeled to follow.

45

Colonel Tibbet didn't know who the young Indian was that sat astride the appaloosa mare, and didn't really give a damn, but whatever the young man had said, seemed to have made a difference. Never having been one to lose an opportunity, Tibbet moved his mount around and started back the direction they'd come from.

As he passed his junior officer he said, smugly, "Major Redding, you take command of the prisoner detail." At that he urged his mount forward confident the soldiers would follow.

The Kid watched as Mose swung down from his pony and stepped over to Noch-ay-del-Klinne. He took the man by the arm, talking to him. Noch-ay-del-Klinne was confused, Mose was explaining that they were leaving now.

Noch-ay-del-Klinne shook his head, trying to tell Mose that he wasn't ready. He needed to collect some of his things. He had to have someone bring his pony.

The Kid nudged his pony closer to Redding, beside the bearded scout Booker. "Appears your colonel is anxious to go," he said mildly.

Booker looked at him, then swiveled his head. Sure enough,

Colonel Tibbet was moving to the outskirts of the camp, heading for the creek crossing, moving further and further away. With the wave of his hand, a relieved D troop began to follow him. The pack train did the same.

"Jesus Christ," Booker swore. He turned back to Mose, his voice loud with fear, "Tell the man to come on, we're getting left behind!"

Mose shrugged, still holding Noch-ay-del-Klinne's arm. In his broken English he said, "We wait for his horse." He indicated the lodge. "The woman is gathering his things."

Booker looked around the camp, his eyes wider, "Well, let's go man!" The Kid looked for Gar, knowing if there was trouble, it would come from him. The man had disappeared. John Daisy sat, patiently waiting for Nalin to reappear. Tibbet and his troop were moving further and further away. The little colonel had not so much as glanced behind him. While D troop and the pack train moved out of the camp, C troop was left waiting. Every trooper was now cursing the little colonel, many not understanding what the hell was happening. It was a July day, and the sun was out, but if it had been in the dead of a freezing winter, the men of C troop would still be wet with sweat.

As the last of the pack train moved away from the center of the camp, the gap was filled with Apaches. Mostly men, bare to the waist, and many now wore the paint of their fathers. Most of these men were armed. They waited with no sound. In their midst was Gar.

The troop stood two abreast in a line that was from the fire pit back toward the south. Toward the end of the column, one of the troopers leaned forward and whispered a name to the man closest to him. The other man leaned toward him, not understanding. The trooper whispered, "It's my real name, if I don't make it out and you do, let my people know."

Finally, two ponies were brought up. Nalin had come from the wickiup carrying a bundle. Without hurry, she secured it to her pony and Mose helped Noch-ay-del-Klinne onto the back of the other mount. Nalin stayed on the ground.

The Kid noticed that the old man seemed to falter. Mose struggled in helping the man up on the back of his horse. By now, Booker had pulled his pistol and Major Redding had to order him to holster it. Impatiently, Redding signaled the column forward and finally they began to move.

As one of her followers led her horse, Nalin stepped out ahead of her father's pony and accompanied with little dance steps, her voice raised in a chant of prayer. From a pouch she took handfuls of holy ground meal and cast it, side to side, before the horses. The women close by took up the chant, moving up beside her. Noch-ay-del-Klinne sat astride his pony, eyes on the horizon, his mouth softened by pride for the young girl.

Troop C was now surrounded by a chanting throng. Major Redding was not certain whether the Apaches would let them through. Sensing his hesitation, Lieutenant Gatewood moved up beside him, quietly urging him to keep the troop moving forward. The major, bolstered by the quiet confidence of the lieutenant, found his voice and urged the troop onward. For a brief moment the Apaches appeared not ready to give way. The Kid and John Daisy moved up beside Nalin and the line of warriors gave ground. As the two men bracketed the Indian girl the crowd opened, allowing a path. The column moved forward, led by the big appaloosa.

The troop moved at a steady and unhurried pace. As they neared the creek, Noch-ay-del-Klinne began to cry out in a loud and insistent voice. He was calling to the major, wanting his attention. Major Redding heard and signaled a halt. He stopped and looked back to the medicine man. With a wave of the hand, he signaled Mose to bring the man forward. It was then that Nalin ceased chanting and as one of the women brought her pony up, she swung up on it, moving it up beside her father.

The small diyin' was talking rapidly to Mose. Mose explained to the major, "Noch-ay-del-Klinne asks that the troop be detoured along the water here. He says that his people have planted a patch of corn and if we cross here, we will trample it."

The young major turned to Lieutenant Gatewood. "What do you think, Lieutenant?"

Gatewood shrugged, "Shallow creek, there'll be plenty of places to cross."

The Kid had pulled his pony up beside the appaloosa, wondering, as the rest, what the medicine man wanted. Suddenly John Daisy touched the Kid's arm. With a nod, John Daisy indicated a spot across the creek.

There sat Gar and a dozen braves.

"What the hell do ya think he's gonna do?" the Kid asked.

John Daisy shrugged.

"Do you think he's deliberately tryin' to get Noch-ay-del-Klinne killed?"

John Daisy's face was hard, "Gar no longer thinks of Noch-ay-del-Klinne. Gar

now thinks only of Gar."

220

46

The Major signaled the troop forward, in the new direction, and the entire mass of people began moving again. In a few minutes, the column was out of the camp, and they began to pick up speed. Many of the Apaches, on foot, began to trail behind. Except for the sound of the horses moving through the grass, there was nothing else to hear. An eerie silence had fallen and many a trooper would describe this day as the most unnerving of his life.

The intermingled mass of blue-coated soldiers and half-naked Apaches moved along the direction of the flowing water. No one was certain of what the next minutes would bring. Neither knew where this day was headed. The one thing they all shared was a desire to get out of here alive. For the troopers, a wish to see the fort again. For the Apache, a need to be able to live a life they considered normal. Oh, only to be normal.

The intermingled mass moved north, and the afternoon faded quickly with the sun burning its way across the nearly cloudless sky. Although the tension was high the movement became a familiar thing, the two groups eventually knowing that the other was not going to start a bloodletting.

By midafternoon it had become, not a confrontation, but simply, what was happening now. There were a handful of low-slung clouds on the horizon and now their flattened edges began to show a crimson tinge.

As the column crested another rise, out ahead and below, a mile or so, Colonel Tibbet and D troop were bivouacking for the night, seemingly ignorant that almost half of the command was not with them.

Without thinking about it, Major Redding reined his mount to a halt. He studied the scene before him. Gatewood was at his elbow.

"Jesus, look at him," Gatewood muttered. "He thinks he's on a picnic."

In the distance the packers were making camp just off the stream, in front of a stand of trees. It was the only open ground for miles. Gatewood would have approved of that choice. Over on a flat high area the packers were erecting a large white tent. Beside the tent, they had started a large fire.

"It's hotter than hell out here," the major muttered. He swept his campaign hat off and wiped his forehead with his sleeve. He had to laugh. He shook his head, "He's going to have an officer's mess!" He was incredulous, he laughed again, shaking his head.

Gatewood said, "He thinks he's on a goddam lark."

The major nodded. "That's exactly what he thinks." He glanced back behind him. "He's over there writing his own headlines. Figuring this will make him famous. Chasing down a broken-down old Apache medicine man." He placed his campaign hat back on his head. "He doesn't even know he's separated his command."

The Kid and John Daisy had moved up beside Noch-ay-del-Klinne and Booker. Nalin was a few paces off. They too, looked at the camp being set up below them. John Daisy caught the Kid's eye and with a turn of the head, indicated a spot off to their left.

Across from them, a hundred yards away, Gar sat on the brown and white pony, surrounded by his followers. He still wore the death's head paint on his face, and his spirit shirt.

The Kid nudged his mount up beside the Major. "Major," the Kid said softly. "This here's your party, but if I was Gar and I was gonna make a move, I'd do it before you got hooked up with the rest of them soldier boys."

The major looked over the Kid's shoulder and saw his meaning. He turned to the civilian scout. "Mr. Booker," he ordered. "You and Sergeant Mose take the prisoner out front and get him to the camp quickly."

Booker nodded and started forward. Noch-ay-del-Klinne followed. For some reason Noch-ay-del-Klinne slid off his pony. Maybe to slow things down. Nalin followed suit.

"Lieutenant," the Major continued, "spread the men in a double skirmish line, placing themselves between the prisoner and that group of Indians." With a gloved hand, he indicated Gar and his men.

"Yessir," Gatewood replied, turning to give the order. Down the slope, Booker and Mose had Noch-ay-del-Klinne bracketed and since he was on foot, they used their mounts to herd him like a cow, toward the camp on the creek.

Colonel Tibbet had spent the last half hour mentally practicing the dressing down he was going to give the young major that evening at the officer's mess. He had begun devising the speech when he had finally glanced behind and found his troop alone. He would show the insubordinate young man what it was like to be an officer in this man's army. Let us see how the boy managed his control tonight, the colonel mused.

He had always been irritated that someone so young as Redding had made rank so quickly. He believed that if he dug deeply enough he would find some benefactor, some angel, bringing the boy along. Someone obviously connected. He made a mental note to ask General Carr what he knew about it.

Finally, after what seemed to be much longer than it actually was, he saw C troop crest the hill. He walked out toward the creek, looking past the water as suddenly the top of the slope was filled with more than just the troopers.

"Mother of God," he whispered under his breath.

Two riders and an Apache on foot started toward him ahead of the others, the two riders herding the man ahead of them. Behind them was the figure of the girl hurrying to catch them. C troop suddenly swung out in a double skirmish line, blocking a number of the Apaches from the three riders. Tibbet recognized the Apache on foot as Noch-ay-del-Klinne.

Colonel Tibbet turned and bellowed, "Sergeant Barnes!"

The sergeant was across the camp, working with a squad picketing the remuda. He turned at the colonel's voice. Sensing the urgency, he half ran, half walked across the ground to the man. "Yessir," he gulped, following the colonel's eyes to the oncoming horde.

"Major Redding's coming in," the colonel said evenly. He turned and looked up and down the creek bank. "Set up a squad of men here at the bank. In a skirmish line, sergeant. Carbines at the ready!"

"Yessir," Barnes snapped a salute and turned to carry out the orders.

As the three men came closer, Tibbet watched Booker and the one called Mose trying to keep the old man moving. He kept stopping and they had to urge him forward. Major Redding and his troop were back away and were surrounded on three sides by Apache riders.

Barnes brought his squad up and deployed them in front of the stand of cottonwoods. Each man had his carbine up and loaded. But, even with the number of Apaches in front of him, Tibbet felt no alarm. He had been at the reservation long enough to be lulled into a large distain for these people. He felt that if they were going to attack, they would have done so by now. He knew they were aware of the danger to their holy man if they became hostile. As Booker and Mose and Noch-ay-del-Klinne reached the creek they forded it just a few yards away from the colonel. He watched, satisfied as they came toward him, out of the water. He turned to indicate a small tent he had earlier ordered erected.

"Put the prisoner there, Mr. Booker," he said pointing up the bank.

Booker nodded and reined his horse to push Noch-ay-del-Klinne up the bank.

The colonel watched stonily as Major Redding led C troop in. Lieutenant Gatewood was the last trooper in, and beside him, the long-haired Kid. Twenty yards behind him, and out in front of the mass of Apaches, was the young Apache that had translated in the camp. He rode the huge spotted horse. Next to him was the strikingly beautiful young woman.

225

47

A few feet from the girl stood the troublemaker, Gar, with the hideous black and white paint on his face. This man had just caught up with the other two, and Colonel Tibbet could see that the three of them were in a heated discussion. He couldn't hear them and wouldn't have understood them anyway, but he could see that the translator and the troublemaker were on the verge of fighting. The girl appeared to be trying to keep peace.

As these three moved forward, it dawned on the colonel that they intended to cross the creek and come into camp. The colonel was alarmed. If three came in, they all would come in.

He turned and called quickly, "Mr. Booker, come here please." As Booker strode up, he said, "You speak their language, don't you?"

Booker was looking at the oncoming Apaches. "Some!" he said cautiously.

"How do you tell them to go away. To say *get away*, or *get out*?"

Booker thought about it. "Ugashe'," he said.

Tibbet turned and half ran down the slope, seeing John Daisy and Nalin and Gar entering the far side of the creek. Waving his arms wildly, he ran into the water, shouting, "Ugashe', Ugashe'!"

Up in the camp, the Kid had his back to the creek. Hearing his name, he shied his horse around, the Walker Colt appearing in his hand. John Daisy was startled at the crazy man running out in front of him. He pulled the appaloosa around the man. Nalin had stopped dead in the center of the creek.

Gar was shocked by this hair-faced nantan shouting the name of the hated white child at him. Astonished, he pulled his pony up beside Nalin and sat staring at the man. The man was coming toward him, yelling, "Ugashe'! Ugashe'!

Gar threw his head back and screamed his war cry. He brought his rifle up and shot the crazy hair-face nantan through the chest!

Colonel Tibbet pitched face forward into the water of Cibicue Creek, dead before he was wet. With a yell, Gar slammed his heels into the flanks of his pony and the horse jumped down the stream, hitting the bank at a run. John Daisy immediately had the appaloosa on the heels of the brown and white pony, determined to bring Gar down.

Nalin sat staring in shock at the dead soldier in the water at her feet. She looked up into the camp and saw the big, white scout, Booker, running to her father, his pistol drawn. She remembered the hair-faced nantan's orders and she screamed her father's name, running toward him.

Noch-ay-del-Klinne held his hands palm out, trying to fend off the oncoming scout. Booker fired on the run. The shot severed the middle finger of the 'diyin's hand then hit him in the chest. He was knocked backwards and sat down hard. He rolled to his side.

Almost as one, the line of troopers opened fire. The volley that hit Nalin lifted her off her feet and slammed her onto the waters of Cibicue Creek.

The Kid fired across his body a split second after Booker fired into the small Indian and his shot took the big scout in the upper arm, spinning the man around. The sound of the Kid's shot was swallowed by the sudden roar of gunfire. All of this in only two seconds.

Both sides of the creek had erupted in gunfire. Three of the soldiers by the creek went down. A group of warriors charged the squad protecting the remuda and two more troopers were hit, the horses scattered, screaming in terror. Major Redding stood firing his service revolver at the scattering Apaches. Between shots he called his orders at the top of his lungs. The surprised troopers began to respond, forming skirmish lines, throwing volley after volley across the creek. Although they were badly outnumbered, their disciplined reactions threw the Apaches in disarray.

48

As they raced over the rise at the bend in the creek, John Daisy charged the big mare into the smaller brown and white pony. Both horses and riders went down in a tumble, both men losing their rifles with the jarring impact. The two men bounced hard in the dusty toboso grass. The little horse was screaming, its foreleg shattered.

John Daisy rolled to his feet, empty handed. A cry of rage came from his lips, and he threw himself across the ground at Gar. Gar responded by leaping forward, his face twisted with rage. The two men slammed into each other, and the force of the impact tumbled them down the rocky slope to the water's edge. Both men attacked bare handed with the ferocity of a wild thing. Head against head, muscle against muscle. Teeth slashing and elbows and fists pounding at each other. It was savagely brutal.

Both men were covered with blood, their skin and hair torn, but neither man seemed to have the advantage. They struggled, might against might, at the water's edge. Suddenly shifting his weight, Gar grabbed John Daisy's arm and flung him around, into the water. John Daisy lost his footing and went down. With a cry, Gar leaped into the water on the fallen man with the meaty sound of flesh tearing flesh. John Daisy pushed backwards, to deeper water, struggling to his feet, suffering the blows that Gar was raining on his head and neck. Gar managed to hook a heel behind John Daisy and John Daisy went down again, heavily, crashing through the water onto the smooth rounded stones that lined the bottom of the creek bed. Reaching into the water, Gar came up with a stone the size of melon. As John Daisy struggled to regain his footing, Gar raised the stone over his head, poised to smash it against the skin and bone of the other man. He brought it down hard. In desperation, John Daisy shifted, kicking out. The kick slammed against the side of Gar's knee and as the rock smashed into the point of John Daisy's shoulder, he felt Gar's knee buckle sideways at a sickening angle. John Daisy felt his arm go numb and he fell back into the water.

Gar's leg buckled and he went down. His arm dangling, John Daisy rolled on top of Gar, using his weight to hold the man down. With his good hand, he forced Gar's painted face deep into the water. Gar struggled violently, pushing up with all his might. He succeeded in breaking the surface for air.

John Daisy knew he couldn't keep the powerful man down with just one arm. He rolled suddenly to his side and slid his good arm around Gar's neck. The man was gagging and spitting. He wrapped his legs around Gar's torso and twisted them both to Gar's bad side. Gar's injured leg crumpled and now they were both under water. John Daisy buried his face into the man's shoulder and squeezed Gar's windpipe with all of his strength. Going in, he had filled his lungs, Gar was coughing.

Gar's struggle to get to his feet was gigantic, but his one leg was useless. He tried to force them both back up to the air, but every time he got his good leg under them, John Daisy would trip him, holding him down.

John Daisy's head was filled with blood and his ears began to pound. Still, he held on, squeezing with all of his might. His chest began to heave, desperately craving air, and still he held on. Bright spots exploded just behind his eyelids, and everything was going black. He found himself clawing his way to his feet, coughing and retching. He turned to prepare himself for Gar's onslaught, but Gar's lifeless body floated face down a yard away. For a long moment John Daisy stared at the body of his longtime rival. Then, he threw his head back and howled like a wolf.

49

After the initial explosion of gunfire, the firing gradually tapered until it had become sporadic. It had been brief and destructive, but now it was mostly gone. The troopers had taken control of the stand of trees and the position of the encampment afforded a good field of fire. On the other side the Apaches were leaderless and in confusion. Many wanted to simply return to their camp, others wanted the blood of the soldiers.

And now, the word came that as Gar had fled around the bend, Chan-Deisi had caught him and killed him. There were some that wanted to now kill Chan-Deisi, but most of the others blamed Gar for the slaying of Noch-ay-del-Klinne and his daughter. Most all concluded that the spirit shirts were not the magic Gar had promised, and most of the warriors stripped them off and cast them away.

As the firing died down, the Kid rose from his crouched position. He had fired only the one shot, and Booker had suffered its result. He replaced the spent cartridge and holstered his pistols. The scout was propped against the small tent that had been intended to house the prisoner. He was unconscious, bleeding to death. The bullet had severed an artery. The Kid looked at him with cold eyes, feeling only regret that he had not fired a split second sooner. It crossed the Kid's mind that the soldiers might take exception to having their civilian scout killed, but, apparently, in the initial explosion of gunfire, no one had noticed how the scout had come to be shot.

The Kid looked out across the front of the camp and there were several blue-coated bodies scattered in the sandy dirt. Across the creek, he could count at least a dozen downed Apaches. In the water, the colonel's body had drifted downstream a dozen yards, and was caught in the roots of a towering oak. Nalin was still where she had fallen. Her pony had found her and was obediently standing beside her.

The Kid unbuckled his gun belt and let his pistols drop to the ground. Taking his hat and holding it into the air, he started slowly down the slope to the water's edge. Behind him someone, he thought it was Redding, called, "Hold your fire!"

The Kid walked slowly into the water and the sun touched the crimson horizon. Replacing his hat, he looked down into the water at the beautiful girl. The crystal water fanned her hair out and her eyes were closed as if she were just sleeping. The blood from her wounds had been washed away and only the torn buckskin dress indicated where her life had been torn from her.

The Kid felt a pain that would never go away. His eye was taken to something shiny, under the water, around her neck. As he leaned down and lifted her from Cibicue Creek he could see it was Miss Lucy's silver locket.

He lifted Nalin's dripping body from the water and carried her up the bank. He lay her in the sandy grass and gently smoothed the hair from her face. With shaking hands, he unsnapped the clasp on the locket and lifted it to the light. He opened the face of the tiny thing and looked at the exquisite likeness of Shonto Page's mother.

He snapped the locket shut and put it into his pocket. He looked up to see the soldiers watching him. He glanced back over his shoulder and there were many Apaches, many of whom were old friends, standing in the waning light, watching.

Behind him, he heard a pony walking in the water. He had heard the cry of the wolf and he knew who came now. His heart was heavy, and he turned slowly, not wishing to have to look into the face of his brother, John Daisy.

50

Ochocama, old Nino, and a dozen others came to John Daisy as he stood over Nalin's body. Ochocama spoke quietly to John Daisy and John Daisy nodded. He and the Kid and the rest gathered up the bodies of Nalin and her father then rapidly took them away from the creek and up to a bluff that overlooked the water. John Daisy insisted they hide the bodies for fear they would be mutilated. There wasn't the normal time for tradition, and they worked fervidly to cover all the tracks so the graves would never be found.

When they were done the Kid stood beside John Daisy and waited. John Daisy's grief was deep and black and for a long time the Kid didn't think his friend would speak. But he finally did.

His voice was soft and barely heard over the distant rushing of the waters. "My grandfather cannot go to the reservation. He says many are going back and many others plan on attacking the blue-coats at Fort Apache."

"What do we do?" the Kid said, leaving it entirely up to John Daisy.

John Daisy was looking into the distance. It took a while

before he spoke. "I will take Ochocama into the Madres and try to settle him there. He just wants to live out his life in peace. These others want to go with him."

"I will go with you," the Kid said.

"No. You must go with the blue-coats and help the young major. He will need you."

"You will need me."

"He will need you more. He is in command now. Tibbet and Booker are dead, the scouts are scattered. He will need your knowledge."

The Kid was quiet. He looked at the sky. "It will be dark soon. If I am to go, I need to go now. The same with you."

John Daisy nodded. He turned and for the first time in his life, the Kid saw tears in his brother's eyes. They embraced and the Kid swung up on his horse. He walked it to where Ochocama was seated. They looked at each other.

"I go now, Grandfather," he said. "Chan Deisi will take you to the Madres."

"I wish you well," Ochocama said.

The Kid didn't trust himself to say anything more. He turned his mount and rode away.

51

The idlers that normally spent their days sunning and spitting and whittling on the plank-board porches along Whiskey Row were aroused from their lethargy by the attention the new posted addition of the Prescott Weekly Journal was receiving.

Usually, when Ben Wright posted the paper on the board at the front of his print shop, most everyone would stop to look at it, but today it had drawn a crowd. Ben Wright was proud of this story. He knew it would be a sensation even as he gleaned the meager bits of information from the offices of General Carr. His old friend John Thompson at the Denver Nugget had picked it up and he was sure some of the prestigious eastern papers were running it also. Beneath the masthead, was a line of bold type:

MASSACRE ON CIBICUE CREEK
another Little Big Horn?

The story went on to read: *"Early reports indicate that Troops C and D of Fort Apache, under the command of Colonel E. G. Tibbet, were savagely attacked by hordes of renegade Indians. The Indians were illegally off the San Carlos reservation.*

Sources say that the Apaches had followed a self-style 'Messiah' into the Cibicue region to perform what was referred to as 'pagan dances.' It is believed by Army sources that there have been many casualties and only a handful of our brave protectors made it back to the safety of Fort Apache under the cover of darkness.

The troops, serving under the orders of General Carr, were sent to apprehend a renegade medicine man. It is believed that the man was influenced by his knowledge of the life of Jesus Christ and believed himself to be the savior of his people. Unconfirmed reports state that casualties of this barbaric bloodshed include the medicine man, and the brave and heroic Colonel E. G. Tibbet. The total number of casualties is currently unknown.

A few days later Ben put up a follow-up, which also caused a sensation:

A FOLLOW UP TO THE CIBICUE MASSACRE
A Tale of Our Heroic Soldiers

Reports from Fort Apache tell this newspaper that at the Cibicue Creek Massacre a number of our valiant troopers were killed – a list of names and particulars will follow after families have been notified. We are told there were far fewer brave troopers slain than the number of savages that met their demise. The reports say that a huge number of the savages followed our troops back to Fort Apache intent on murder, but due to the bravery of a scout, whose name is unavailable, and the exemplary leadership showed by the officers, all troopers arrived safely. What followed was a number of attacks on the fort but now the word from the reservation is that the majority of the renegades are trickling back to the reservation and the Fort is no longer under attack.

The winter turned into a bad one and the soldiers at the fort only ventured forth to repair the telegraph lines and chop wood. It was a month after the spring thaw that the Kid moved his mount down the long slope and rode toward the hazy smoke that lay like a blanket on the town of Prescott. The town hadn't changed much since he had been there. It had rained recently, and the streets were mud. Not sloppy, but still mud.

He stopped at the hotel on the square and procured a room. After he had carried his possibles, including the Walker Colt, up to the room, he dropped his mount at the livery that was closest to Miss Lucy's saloon. Carrying his rifle in its beaded and fringed sheath across the back of his neck he walked to Miss Lucy's.

There was a new bartender. This time he relinquished the rifle and his side pistol as he took a place at the bar. The place wasn't very busy. The bartender poured his requested beer and set it in front of him. Miss Lucy had put in new stools. She figured that sitting men didn't cause as much trouble as standing men. He stepped up on one and drank half the beer in two swallows. He swung around and surveyed the room. He had always thought that Miss Lucy's was the finest looking saloon in America. Of course, he hadn't seen all the saloons in America, but Shonto had told him of some back east that sounded mighty fine. He was partial to this one.

There were two other men at the bar. Both looked like miners. A man in finer clothes sat at a table at the back by himself. He shuffled and reshuffled a deck of cards. With a smile he nodded at the Kid and the Kid nodded back. Maybe later he'd play some poker, but now he just wanted to sit and drink his beer.

He was on his second one when he saw the cardsharp look

toward the stairs. Molly Sand was coming down. The Kid swiveled to watch her, and her eyes were on him. All the other eyes in the room were on her.

She came down the stairs, hesitated a moment, then crossed the room. He started to say something, but before it could come out, she threw her arms around his neck and kissed him full on the mouth.

The two miners stood with mouths agape, as did the bartender. The poker player had on his best poker face. She finished her kiss, then pulled away. She looked at him then kissed him again. This time he was prepared.

She broke it off and slid up next to him. She waved a hand at the bartender. "Give me a mescal, Joe," she said. She turned back to the Kid.

"I was worried sick about you," she said. "They were saying the whole troop was massacred and I knew you were there."

Joe set the mescal in front of her. She tossed it back and signaled for another. She turned toward him and smacked him on the arm. "Goddam you, you could have let me know you were okay."

"I didn't think you cared."

She laughed. "That just shows you don't much about women. You sweep a girl off her feet to kiss her, then ride away, that girl's going to be thinking about you."

The Kid was looking at her and she was just about the most beautiful woman he'd ever seen. "I've got something for you," he said. He pulled the small medicine pouch from his belt and opened it. He rummaged inside, then pulled out the locket and let it dangle.

Molly sucked her breath in. Her eyes welled and she couldn't speak. She gently took it into her hands. When she could speak, she said, "I'd do anything for that woman. I'd give her my life and when she gave me this locket to get cleaned I lost it." Her voice tailed off. She gathered herself. "When I lost it, I'd just as soon died." She wiped the tears from her eyes. "I knew you'd find it for me." She slid off the stool, "Come on, let's go give it to her." She handed him the locket. "You give it to her."

She took the Kid's hand and pulled him behind her as she crossed the room and went up the stairs. The door to Miss Lucy's apartment was shut. Molly rapped on it in a distinctive staccato pattern.

Miss Lucy's faint voice came through the door. "Come."

Molly opened the door and stepped in. Miss Lucy was sitting by the window embroidering. She didn't look up.

"I've got something for you," Molly said.

"Hold on," Miss Lucy said, frowning with concentration. She finally finished the stitch and looked up. Molly moved out of the way and pulled the Kid into the room.

"Kid," said Miss Lucy, surprised. She set her work aside and stood. She held her arms out to him. The Kid moved across the room and embraced Miss Lucy. They held each other for a long time.

"I knew no number of Apaches would get any kid of Shonto Page's," she said into his shoulder.

"Show her what you brought her," Molly said.

The Kid stepped back and held his hand out. He let the locket drop and dangle by its chain.

Miss Lucy took it into her hand. She opened it, then with

loving care shut it again. She looked at the Kid. "This means the world to me," she said. "He dropped me here and gave me this just before he rode away."

52

The Kid was playing poker when the day coach driver came in after a run and washed the dust from his throat with glasses of beer. After two, he brought the third over to where the Kid was playing cards.

He stood watching a moment, then said to the Kid, "Saw your Indian friend at Del Norte's when we came through."

Forty minutes later, the Kid had said goodbye to Molly Sand and Miss Lucy, gathered his things and after a couple of stops was riding out of town. When it got too dark to travel, he made camp beside the road with a small fire and a pot of coffee. He ate jerky and cold beans and rolled into his blanket early. He was up before dawn and fed his mount from the bag of grain he had bought at the livery.

He reached Del Norte's when the sun was high. The road angled up a long slope and at the top you could see a mile. There was a low swale ahead and beyond it the road rose again into another long upward rise. Smack in the middle of the swale was Del Norte's. Positioned for no surprises. Handmade over the years with mud and straw bricks and sporting several rooms, each added in the monsoon time, so mud bricks were easier to make. There was a barn and two corrals, one for Del Norte's private stock and the other to hold the day-wagon team overnight. For the comfort of the travelers Del Norte had put in two outhouses. One a two holer, for the gents, and the other with polished wood and a single hole for the ladies. Woe be to the traveling drummer who thought he deserved the single hole. He would immediately suffer the wrath of Juh, the good-sized wife of Del Norte. Juh was the eldest daughter of Ochocama and she and Del Norte had been left in peace for many years.

The Kid sat for a long moment and studied the place and all the land around it. He gently nudged his pony down the slope. By the time he was down the slope they were waiting for him. Del Norte hadn't changed much, maybe a little more bandy-legged but his shoulder-length hair was still full and white. As was his beard. Juh was smiling broadly. John Daisy stood to the side.

The Kid reached behind himself to his bag and pulled out a sack. He tossed it to Del Norte. "Brought you some city-bought tobacco "

"Well, I'm much obliged," said Del Norte.

The Kid pulled another package out and handed it to Juh. She opened it and pulled out four small wheels of colored ribbon. She beamed.

The Kid stepped down from his pony and John Daisy took the reins. "What did you bring me?" John Daisy said.

"Me," said the Kid.

"I've got the stew pot on," Juh said. "You hungry?"

"Always," the Kid said.

John Daisy started walking the pony back to the barn. The Kid trailed along.

When they reached the barn, the Kid looked around and said, "Where's the appaloosa?"

John Daisy stopped walking and turned. His eyes went to the far south mountains. A western breeze brought in the soft sweet smell of new sage and creosote blossoms rising in the air. John Daisy finally turned to look at the Kid. "One of us had to be free," he said.

The End

Did you enjoy
Shadow Dancer?

If you enjoyed this book. Go to Amazon.com, search for the book then click on the reviews and leave one. Thanks for reading.

You can go online to leave a review at the address below, or for more acclaimed novels by Sam Lee Jackson.

www.samleejackson.com

Made in the USA
Columbia, SC
30 December 2021

52770090R00152